The Other Side of Haight

The Other Side of Haight

A NOVEL

James Fadiman

Celestial Arts
Berkeley Toronto

This is a work of fiction. Names, places, characters, and incidents are either the products of the author's imagination or are used fictitiously, and any resemblance to events, locales, or actual persons, living or dead, is entirely coincidental.

CELESTIAL ARTS P.O. Box 7123 Berkeley, California 94707 www.tenspeed.com

Distributed in Canada by Ten Speed Press Canada, in the United Kingdom and Europe by Airlift Books, in New Zealand by Southern Publishers Group, in Australia by Simon & Schuster Australia, in South Africa by Real Books, and in Singapore, Malaysia, Hong Kong, and Thailand by Berkeley Books.

Cover and text design by George Mattingly at Studio GMD, using Blue Island and Eric Gill's Joanna.

Cover photograph by Elaine Mayes. Digitally altered with permission of the photographer.

LIBRARY OF CONGRESS CATALOGING-IN-PUBLICATION DATA

Fadiman, James, 1939–
        The other side of Haight : a novel / James Fadiman.
            p. cm.
        ISBN 0-89087-984-2
            1. Haight-Ashbury (San Francisco, Calif.)—Fiction. 2. San Francisco (Calif.)—Fiction.
    3. Drug use—Fiction. 4. LSD (Drug)—Fiction. 5. Hippies—Fiction. I. Title.
        PS3556.A315 O8 2001
        813'.54—dc21
                                    00-043195

First printing, 2001

Printed in the United States of America

1 2 3 4 5 6 7   05 04 03 02 01

For Dorothy,
more than my wife, more than my inspiration.
And for so many others
who, when they wished to,
could make the sun stand still,
just for the joy of it.

There is

light enough

for those who wish

to see,

and

darkness enough

for those of the

opposite disposition.

Blaise Pascal

PART I

CHAPTER 1

Wrong side of the border

*The human soul needs actual beauty
even more than bread.*

D. H. Lawrence

October 1, 1966

San Francisco

SOME MORNINGS, when Sweeps walked to work stoned, the Haight seemed like a ghost town and depressed him. Today, however, walking the empty streets under a sky still pearl gray with early light, his only concern was what to do with Canada Frank.

Frank had been living in the cellar for more than a week, and refused to leave it except to eat. Hiding from his draft board, he told them. But he was Canadian. Sweeps had met guys evading the draft who passed through the Haight on their way to Canada, but never the other way around. Something had turned Canada Frank's brains into scrambled eggs.

Inside the ballroom, it was so quiet that all Sweeps could hear was the hiss of his dust mop sliding along the wood floor and the rustle of paper and other scraps bouncing along in front of the mop head. Noticing a partly smoked joint, he bent down, picked it up and slid it gently into his right pants pocket.

He shook his mop out through a low window into the alley. Gray and brown dust mixed with face powder, body-paint flakes, pot seeds and specks of tobacco to form a multicolored cloud that drifted down onto the cracked pavement. Sweeps pulled the mop back in and continued to plough his way up and down the floor, creating a clean stripe on every pass.

He picked up a dime from behind a chair leg and put it in his left pocket. He'd tell Frank that it was safe to come over here. It would be good for Frank to get out. He could watch Sweeps work. "In the morning," he'd tell him, "the fuzz and the folks are all deep asleep."

Sweeps thought it was bizarre to hide from the wrong army on the wrong side of the border. He didn't like to think about what he went through to dodge his draft call. A raucous chorus of "Onward Christian Soldiers" struck up inside his head. He focused on moving the mop to shut out the unwelcome music.

It took three days to cajole Frank out of the cellar. Sweeps put piles of soap boxes and rags into a pair of buckets. He told Frank that without his help, it would take an extra trip to get all the stuff over there. "Just carry one damn bucket!" he said. Frank hesitated. Only when Moonflower put her arms around him and said, "No helpee, no eatee," did Frank finally agree.

All the way over, Frank kept looking behind him, double-checking every moving car. As they entered the ballroom, he was still shaking his head back and forth and talking to himself. After prowling through the whole building, Frank perched on the edge of a chair far from the doors, his hands stuffed into his pockets and legs pressed together, his eyes tracking the moving mop. Sweeps saw how the mop's gliding motion began to tow Frank's mind along like a dinghy behind a sailboat. Eventually, Frank slid back in the chair and seemed to unwind a little.

From time to time, Sweeps looked over, wondering if Frank would ask for a turn like girls almost always did when he brought them along. Sweeps jabbed at a piece of gum stuck to the floor. Taking out his pocket knife, he scraped it up and uncovered a nickel. He cut away the dried gum and flashed the coin at Frank before putting it in his pocket. Frank gave Sweeps a little high sign with his thumb.

Sweeps pulled an almost perfect joint out from under a chair cushion. It smelled of perfume. Some college dolly too scared to smoke. He rolled the joint back and forth between his thumb and first finger. No seeds or stems—first-class stuff.

As they walked back, Sweeps asked Frank where he'd come from. After looking around to see if anyone was nearby, Frank spoke in a very low voice. "There are lots of small islands off Vancouver. Some have villages, some just a few houses. A few got no people at all. I hid on one after I run away from the hospital. In the mornings I'd go down to the beach with a knife."

"What for?"

"Oysters! Low tide. Pry them loose, cut 'em open. Spit on 'em. Ones that squirm, you eat. They taste salty, feel like slime. When you bite down, the insides mix with the muscle—that's mostly what they are."

Sweeps suppressed a shudder.

"I'd stand there in water up to my ankles and eat two dozen. Carry me most of the day.

"Saw an owl one night—big-eyed mother. Scared the pee out of me. That night I was afraid even to build a fire. But I knew I could find enough berries and—" Suddenly Frank stopped and pointed. "Look!"

A man wearing a dark overcoat and matching hat was getting out of a cab in front of a three-story Victorian four or five houses away. The doorway moldings were sharply outlined in blue and white trim, and the top floor windows were rose- and lavender-tinted stained glass. The driver unloaded a large leather suitcase and a matching smaller one from the trunk. The man paid his fare and the cab pulled away.

Sweeps whistled through his teeth. "That's no hotel. It's a cat house."

"It's Langwater," Frank said in a hushed voice. He shrank behind Sweeps into the shallow doorway of the Print Mint. When the door of the Victorian opened, the man picked up his suitcases and went inside.

"Hey, man, he's gone," Sweeps said. "He's come to get a piece of ass, but not yours."

Frank remained frozen.

"Oh, come on." Sweeps reached out his hand.

Frank bolted past Sweeps like a greyhound coming out of the gate. "I never should have come with you," Frank hollered over his shoulder. "I'm fucked, royally fucked! He's come to take me back."

Back in the house, Frank made straight for the cellar and locked himself in. Sweeps hung up his cleaning tools and went to his own room. He ducked his head going through the low doorway and waved at the Ted Williams poster on the far wall that proclaimed:

If you don't think too good, don't think too much.

He lifted the worn copy of the I Ching off his pillow and lay on his mattress, staring up at the small sloping window. Frank is truly crazy. If we'd left a minute later, nothing to sweat about. But what do I know, maybe anything would have set him off.

In the cellar, Canada Frank whimpered. He struggled against the nurse giving him the injection. The other nurses stood around his bed laughing. One pointed to his penis, which was getting smaller and smaller. He tried to reach for it but found that they'd strapped him down. He wanted to scream but didn't. He was afraid Dr. Langwater would hear him and punish him again.

In the living room of the Victorian, David Langwater, M.D. met with the assembled research team. He did not hide his displeasure with the rate of progress or his irritation with the staff's defensiveness.

Two days later, Nitrous Eddie ran up the stairs. "Up! Up!" he shouted. "Spring has sprung. Eden has returned to River City. There is an excess of joy in Mudville! Arise, you louts and loutesses. See the day that God hath wrought."

Behind her closed door, Moonflower shouted, "Eddie, shut the fuck up."

"Our house is our castle. Home is where the heart is. The family that smokes together jokes together."

Sweeps pulled his door open. Eddie was hopping back and forth on the landing. "Eddie, for god's sake, what is it?"

"You don't know? You really don't." Eddie stopped his dance and looked at Sweeps. "Canada Frank has crept out—to find himself a new paranoid haven. We are free of his dark cloudness. Also his piggy appetite."

"You sure?" Sweeps barely concealed a yawn.

"Would I trouble my friends with a will-o'-the-wisp rumor? Would I lie? Scratch the second question. His hideout is bare. Not a trace that he sucked upon us—not a matchstick, nor a gum wrapper, probably not a fingerprint."

From behind her door Moonflower said, "Hip, hip, hooray. Now shut up or I'll have your balls for breakfast."

Eddie scampered downstairs. "Yes, my big-breasted thrush," he called. "I hear and obey." He ran down the hall and into the living room, yipping cheerfully to himself.

CHAPTER 2

Never trust anybody

Do not struggle to understand.
If through weakness
you are attracted to thinking,
you will have to wander
amidst this world of existence
and suffer pain.

The Tibetan Book of the Dead

October 8, 1966
San Francisco

ANGELO BORDEN OPENED THE DOOR to a beefy red-haired man wearing a brown workshirt and matching pants. A brown baseball cap, pushed back on his head, displayed a woven patch of the Bay Bridge with "City of San Francisco" in a circle around it.

"Good morning. You live here?" the man asked.

"Yes, sir. I mean I've just moved in." Angelo didn't want to explain that he'd only been in the house a few days. "I'm a student."

"That's great, but not to me. Is the owner home?"

"My boss is in the back. Can I help you?"

"I'm with the Fire and Safety Commission. We check these older

houses every few years for conditions that might be dangerous."

Angelo stammered. "I wasn't told…"

"There's no charge. You pay taxes, you get the service." He looked down at a clipboard he was holding. "You're actually overdue."

"Wait a minute." Angelo left the man standing in the foyer. When he couldn't find Bear in the house, he called out, "Be right back."

Going next door, Angelo walked quickly down a darkened hall. Through a partly closed door he heard Bear's voice.

"Excuse me," Angelo said, leaning in.

"What is it, kid?" Bear asked sourly.

"There's an inspector next door."

"What's he want?"

"He says we're overdue for a fire and safety inspection."

Bear's gaze clouded over. "I've dealt with bastards like him in New York and Boston. Fucking graft artists. Get him out of here! Tell him— shit!

"Tell him we been inspected last month. If he gives you lip, ask for his ID." Bear turned to the man sitting across from him. "If he's not shaking us down, that'll be jake with him."

Bear's visitor took out a silver cigarette case and clicked it open. "This city, surprising as you may find it, does not like to have its houses burn down. I bet he's legit."

Bear glared. "Money on it?" He glanced at Angelo. "Get going, kid."

Angelo scuttled back. The inspector was digging at the door fram with a small screwdriver.

"You've got dry rot."

Angelo's words tumbled out. "I asked my boss. He said we've l our inspection. Last month. And he said, th- thank you for coming a way."

The man's eyebrows went up. "I don't think he got it right. neighborhood ain't been inspected for years." He stood squarely i doorway, his shadow extending halfway down the hall.

Angelo shifted from one foot to the other. "He said that, uh, maybe your records might not be right. He asked me to get your name and. . ." He hesitated. "Identification."

"Why don't you give me your boss's name instead?" The man glared at Angelo. "I'll do the calling. You can't stop a city inspection."

Angelo fidgeted. "I'm just saying what he told me."

"You'll be hearing from us! There are penalties for this kind of thing." The man pointed at the door. "And fix the dry rot before that door falls off its hinges."

Later that afternoon Bear called Angelo in. He had his hand over the mouthpiece of the phone.

"Kid, it's for you—cops."

Angelo took the phone. A gruff voice spoke into his ear.

"This is Officer Martin. You the one who met the guy calling himself an inspector?"

"Yes, sir."

"He's a con man. Gets into homes, cases them, comes back later to rob the place. Did you get a good look at him?"

"Yes, sir. I think so."

"Great. I'll send a detective over to get a description."

"Yes, sir. I mean officer."

"You could be a real help." The man hung up.

Bear stood behind his desk, hands on his hips like a washerwoman. "Well, was I wrong! Apologies, young hotshot. Not an inspector shaking us down but a fucking thief." He smirked. "Learn something, kid. No one who comes to your door comes to help you." Bear eased his bulk back into his chair and chuckled, a sound Angelo would have sworn Bear was incapable of.

As he went back up to his work space off the kitchen, Angelo wondered if it had been a mistake to come out here. He could still feel his mother's disconcerting tears on his shirt and his father's forceful handshake just before Angelo boarded the plane from JFK for Los Angeles. At

the last minute his father arranged for him to buy a used car from a second cousin in North Hollywood. The drive north made him a day late, but the letter hadn't said there was any urgency, just to be there by the beginning of October.

From the moment he turned onto the coast road at Santa Monica, the long stretches of white beaches backed by high bluffs and treeless hills, the houses pressed tightly together along the edges of the cliffs, even the open convertibles crowded with suntanned girls—it all felt foreign and exotic. He turned away from the ocean only when the highway turned in toward Goleta, and he was delighted to be returned to it at Pismo Beach. After being advised at a Texaco station that the coast road was being worked on north of San Simeon, he drove reluctantly through San Luis Obispo. There he entered another climate and another world. On the hillsides, nothing green at all, as if the land was gripped by drought, while on the level valley floor row after row of flourishing crops passed in a blur. By the time Angelo stopped at an A&W in King City, he'd become weary of the hazy vistas. He was glad to see tree-covered hills as he drove past San Jose. Nearing San Francisco, he watched vast white waves of fog pouring over the coastal hills like swiftly moving glaciers. "Angelo," he said to himself, "you're not in Kansas anymore, that's for damn sure."

101 to the Fell exit. Fell to Divisidero. Left on D. Right on Haight, Haight to 1801 Hayward.(Two blocks above Haight and one over from Clayton.)

Angelo scrunched the paper into his back pocket, walked up the steps and rang the bell. He waited, looked up to see if anyone was visible through the stained-glass windows and rang again. The door opened a few inches, then clicked against a chain. "What d' ya want?" a man asked.

"Is this the Evergreen Foundation?" Angelo hesitated, suddenly sure he was at the wrong house.

"Why do you want to know?"

"I'm supposed to work for it."

The door closed, the chain rattled and clanked. When it opened again, Angelo faced a man whose thick neck supported a large head and a bulge of jet-black hair. His eyes were so deep set that Angelo couldn't guess their color. The man wore a white shirt open at the throat and a suit coat. He stuffed his hands into the coat's sagging front pockets and looked Angelo up and down. "You the college guy?"

"Yes, sir."

"You're late."

"Well sir, the letter said—" Angelo felt his face redden. "I came in from Los Angeles. I planned to be here yesterday, but my car—"

"Listen, kid. I'm going to tell you a few things. One, nobody has to come up with an alibi when they're on time. Two, I'm in a meeting. Three, if you think I'm not as nice as pie, Dr. David Langwater, your boss and mine, makes me look like a Cub Scout. Want to tell him your story?"

"Yes, sir. I mean no, sir."

"And one last thing, kid. Don't call me sir. It makes me gag."

Angelo stepped back and down one step.

"Move your college-educated ass next door. Say you're with the project. The other college guy—he's waiting for you—he knows the skinny."

Angelo hesitantly extended his hand. "I'm Angelo Borden."

"I'm called Bear." His huge hand reached out and touched Angelo's. "Next door. And kid—Angelo—you don't need a car. Park it away from the house."

"Sure. I'll move it."

Bear leaned toward Angelo. "It's not new, is it?"

"Uh, hardly." He jerked his head, intending to point to the car, but lost his nerve. "It's a sixty-one Plymouth."

Bear shut the door.

Alone on the porch Angelo recalled his father complaining, "I'll be damned if I can figure out why I should pay your full tuition so you can play in San Francisco."

Angelo had taken his time to answer. "Anthropology majors need a semester of field work. I didn't make the rules. But I did pick my location. Howitt'll be in Guatemala living with mosquitoes the size of mice, spiders that eat birds, and native girls who rub their boobs with lard." Angelo was delighted that his father couldn't conceal his disgust.

At this moment, though, Guatemala looked pretty good. Angelo retreated down the steps. At the top of the landing next door, he stood on a worn rectangle of tiny mosaic tiles. There was no bell, only a white hole in the plaster. He banged on the door.

He heard a few quick steps. A young man no older than Angelo, with wide shoulders and a mane of blond hair, opened the door. "Hi. You Norman?"

"Angelo."

"Not Norman?"

"That's a name I never use."

"Great, Angelo." He stuck out his hand. "I'm Brad. We're roommates. Where's your stuff?"

"In the car."

"Good deal. It's a drag here without wheels."

"Bear doesn't seem to think so."

"Bear scare you?"

Angelo nodded.

"He freaks me out," Brad said. "He actually is as mean as he looks."

CHAPTER 3

God opens doors

*We are all messed up
because our heads,
hearts and sex organs
are so far apart.*

Alan Watts

October 8, 1966

L OLLIE ANNE PLACED THE NOTE on the kitchen table under one corner of the glass butter dish. Back in her room, she lay on her quilted bedspread for a long time looking up at the spots on the painted wood of the ceiling.

She had laid out the jeans with "Kiss my patch" sewn on the back pocket, three tops, her blue jacket, her newest panties, two bras, a toothbrush, a hairbrush, strapless gold sandals, a cobalt blue leotard, her swimsuit, eight headbands, and a half-dozen hair clips. Getting up, she stuffed everything into her faded beach bag, decorated with a pale sun shining in a dull sky over greenish-gray coconut palms. She put her library card in the back of her top drawer along with her student identification, then covered them with her senior sweater so the yellow and black timber wolf patch, its jaw biting down on "Turlock High Class of 1966," was face down. She pocketed all of her money, $43.50, and her driver's license.

She hung up everything that had been on the closet floor, pulled her gunmetal gooseneck lamp out from under the desk and put it exactly where her father liked it. She kissed every item on the walls—party and camp pictures, playbills from school productions, the poster of Clark Gable. Stroking Jojo the rabbit, whose eyes were gone, and Tiny Cat, which Mrs. Aubon had given her in preschool, she decided that they were too frayed to travel, so she set them beside the other animals on her bed. She lay down on them and cried for a few minutes. Comforted by her own tears, she took Berry Bear by his neck and stuffed him in the top of the bag beside her jeans.

She walked silently down the stairs, left her house keys on the table and went out the back door, easing it closed so it made only a faint click.

The #2 bus let her off at the downtown station where she boarded the morning bus from Turlock to Modesto. After a half-hour wait in Modesto, she caught an express to San Jose. In San Jose, after almost gagging from the stench in the ladies' room, she seated herself on a torn stool at the bus station's counter. She wolfed down two jelly doughnuts and drank a large Coke before the Santa Cruz bus was called.

Later, when the bus stopped at the top of the mountain at the Cloud Nine Restaurant and the driver went in for coffee, she walked over to the fence at the edge of the parking lot. Below her, she saw ridge after ridge, each with a ragged row of pine trees silhouetted along its crest, falling away into invisibility. Beyond them the Pacific stretched to the horizon like a silver sheet.

"Groovy! Incredibly groovy," she said, and hugged herself.

In the Santa Cruz bus station ladies room, she put her bathing suit on under her clothes. A block from the station, she hitched a ride to the boardwalk. Trying to look casual, she slung her bag over her shoulder and walked down the stairway onto the beach.

On the sand she danced a few steps. "Ta-ta," she said loudly. An elderly woman, her nose bone-white with a layer of zinc oxide, looked up through dark sunglasses, sighed, and returned to her reading. Lollie Anne sniffed the warm wet air like an excited dog, smelling seaweed, dead fish and baby oil. A wave of fatigue and anxiety passed through her. She walked a few more steps and plopped onto the sand.

Her mother's voice rose up in her head. "Take a nap. You'll feel better."

"I'll do what I want!" she snapped, so loudly she startled herself. She stood and took off her shirt and skirt, lay down and wriggled a shallow depression into the sand and put her bag under her head. Gradually the sunlight streaming through her closed lids filled her consciousness with colors. Her pulse pumped the colors in and out of her eyes. She became enmeshed in the brilliance. The warmth worked itself deeper into her body. Sprawled on the sand, she fell into an easy sleep.

Her own shivering woke her. The sky was still bright, but the afternoon fog bank had begun to build offshore and cold air poured onto the beach. Lollie Anne sat up, shook the sand from her hair. She saw that the beach was almost empty. She heard the hollow "twock" of the serve and a slap-slap-slap as players set and slammed the ball in a late volleyball game. She dressed and walked toward the pier, letting the edge of the foam splash over her ankles.

In front of the beach wall, a few people gathered around a fire pit, the flames flaring against the gray concrete. She drifted nearer and sat down where she could see their faces. She drew curve after curve in the sand.

A girl with long, straight hair looked over, met her gaze and smiled. A few minutes later she turned back again and beckoned. "Hey! This fire don't mind if it warms one more. Come on over."

Lollie Anne joined the circle. Grabbing her knees, she gazed straight into the fire. The girl fished out a bun from a string bag and held it toward her. "Want a hot dog? We brought too many."

Lollie Anne started to say "No, thank you," as she'd always been taught, but found herself staring so hard at the bun that she couldn't speak at all. The girl put a hot dog on a stick and handed it to her. "Cook it yourself."

Lollie Anne thrust it into the heart of the fire. After only a moment, she pulled it out, twisted it off the stick with the bun and attacked it in great bites.

"Don't you want mustard?"

"I forgot," she said, her mouth full, still chewing.

"You should never forget what makes things better," the girl said, producing a jar from the bag. "We didn't bring knives. Use your finger."

God! My finger. Right on! Why not? The mustard was warm and grainy. She rubbed it along the hot dog, wiped her finger on the bun and ate the rest without looking up.

"Another?"

She nodded emphatically, grabbing the bun with her free hand. After that one, and a third, she looked up at the girl, who was watching with open fascination. "Starved, weren't you."

"Uh-huh," she said, her mouth still full.

"You from around here?" the girl asked. Her voice seemed as soft as windblown grasses.

Lollie Anne shook her head. "I've been—" She stopped and licked her fingers. "Travelling." She was acutely aware of not knowing what to do or say next. In desperation, she licked her fingers again.

"We're heading back to our place soon. Want to come along?"

Lollie Anne looked around the circle. Her mother's voice started up inside her head like a police siren. "Strangers! Dangers!" But the faces were relaxed and their eyes were clear.

"That'd be great," she said.

"Your folks okay with it?"

"I'm on my own."

"Thought so." The girl touched Lollie Anne's hand. "I'm Maya."

"Lollie Anne." She extended her arm stiffly.

Maya took her outstretched hand and held it softly until Lollie Anne relaxed. "Funny name," she said.

"I hate it."

"I'll try not to use it." Maya relinquished Lollie Anne's hand and lay back on the sand.

"It's nice of you to invite me."

"I thought you might not have a place to go."

"I don't." Tears came to her eyes.

"You do now," Maya said.

One of the men started to sing. The rest joined in. Lollie Anne couldn't get all the words, but the repeated chorus flowed into her. "Santa Cruzing, Santa Cruzing." She let the sounds engulf her. For the first time since she'd left her house, she didn't feel afraid.

Later, in the car, she asked where they lived. "Up Branciforte, in back of the Mystery Spot," said a voice from the front seat.

"Cool," she said, as if she'd understood where that was. Soon she fell asleep, her head bobbing until Maya pulled it onto her shoulder. She was jolted awake when the car bounced along a rough dirt track that went up a hill.

That night and the next she slept on cushions in the living room. On the morning of the third day, she phoned Junie, who yipped like a beagle on hearing her voice.

"I—am—in—bliss!" said Lollie Anne. "I love, love, love it. Call my folks and tell 'em—tell 'em I'm dead. Just kidding. Tell them I'm fine. Really. I'm living with a real band! They write their own music. Incredibly groovy! They found me."

"Where are you?"

"No can do. My folks'd just squeeze it out of you. I'm a runaway. You know, 'Freaked-out teenager vanishes.' Tell Debbie she still owes me that dollar."

Junie let loose a stream of questions, her voice a jumble of concern, envy and adoration.

"It's groovy, incredibly groovy," Lollie Anne said. "I was scared at first. Everyone here is into music."

There was quiet on the line. Then Junie said, "Will you tell me why you left?"

"I can't. Not really."

"Did you—have to?"

"I'm not preg, if that's what you're asking. Jeez Junie, what a question! Dad slapped me sometimes, but nobody knocked me up. Anyway, I miss you—only you."

After hanging up the phone, Lollie Anne went into the kitchen and began washing the glasses in the sink. As she twisted the soapy brush inside each glass, she sang part of a song the band had been rehearsing.

"Did you ever have a feeling?

Ever have a feeling?

That you were in the right place, at the right time.

Did you ever have a feeling?"

A few tiny soap bubbles floating above the sink rainbowed the late-afternoon light.

CHAPTER 4

Ask for Martin

It is with life as with a play—
it matters not how long the action is spun out,
but how good the acting is.

Seneca

THE DETECTIVE WAS MIDDLE-AGED and wore a shabby gray suit, a white shirt and no tie. He seemed to have given up hope of ever looking impressive. "You the one who met the so-called inspector?"

"Yes, sir."

"What happened?"

Angelo told him everything he could remember.

"So you left him standing here while you went next door?"

"Only for a minute or so."

"And where was he when you came back?"

"Still in the doorway."

"Was the door locked while you were gone?"

"No, sir. He was standing in the doorway."

"So you just left him there." The man kept flicking a front tooth with his thumbnail.

"Yes, sir." Angelo flushed.

"Could he have come inside while you were next door?"

"I guess so."

"I guess so, too." The detective sighed, as if he were tired of hearing stories like Angelo's. "Show me where he cut into your door."

"He didn't cut. He poked at it with a screwdriver. He said we had dry rot."

"I bet."

The frame had been painted over so often that it was hard to see the hinge screws. Angelo pointed to some small rectangular depressions. "There. And there."

"Let me see if I can find other places he might have tried."

"Sure."

They went over every downstairs window on the ground floor and even walked outside and clambered around in the extensive crawl space. When they were back in the entryway, the man said, "Maybe you're lucky. He might not have had enough time. But I'd double-check the front door at night. Can you tell me what he looked like?"

Angelo recalled the "inspector's" face clearly. As he spoke, the detective took notes in a little wire-ring notebook he fished out of his jacket pocket. "Could you pick him out of a lineup?"

"I think so, officer."

"You've been a real help." He put the notebook back in his pocket. "Mind if I use your john?"

"No. Go ahead."

Angelo stood in the hallway. He heard the toilet flush and water run in the sink. The door clicked open.

The man walked toward him, still zipping his fly. "If he comes back, stall him. Show him the upstairs, the coal chute. Make up an excuse to leave him. Call SFPD—robbery detail. Ask for Martin."

"Yes, sir." Angelo felt a sudden pleasure at being considered part of a team.

"Top of the morning to you."

Niven put his pad into his pocket and walked to the nearest bus stop. He took a bus to Washington and Larkin, walked half a block and climbed three flights to a clean, freshly painted apartment. He reheated the coffee still on the stove, and made a bologna sandwich with mustard and lettuce. As he sat down at the kitchen table, a key turned in the lock.

"You're home early," Niven said. "That young guy gave you a lovely description. 'Brown eyes with just a touch of green.' A nice detail, I said to myself, Teddy will be pleased."

"Me grandmother had eyes greener than Irish grass. I thought he seemed to be an observant lad," Teddy said as he crossed the room. "The house?"

"Piece of cake. I soaped the window runners in the back john. The latch is easy once you break the glass."

"Worth the trouble?"

"Couple of typewriters, Teddy. Locked desk drawers, nothing on the mantle. No art. I say, go for it. There's something in there worth taking. I can smell it."

"Place empty at night?"

"Don't think so. But the bedrooms are all upstairs. No locks on any of the inside doors." Niven stirred his coffee.

Teddy took off his cap and placed it on the table. "Do they handle cash?"

"Don't be greedy. Taking money is, well, it's like stealing. I think we're just liberating some excess—offering beneficent if unasked for spiritual renunciation."

"Any bologna left?" Teddy asked.

"Help yourself."

"While I do, be a treasure and make us a map."

Teddy put his sandwich together. Niven tore pages out of his note-book, and, spreading them out on the table, proceeded to diagram the layout of the downstairs floor of the house on Hayward, drawing skill-fully and to scale.

CHAPTER 5

Under the spider's web

Welcome to this universe
in which you are a star
in the universal game of
finding who you are.

The Fun Band

THE DAYS MELTED TOGETHER. Every morning, before anyone was up, Lollie Anne restored the living room and cleaned the kitchen. One day she'd make sandwiches and lemonade for everyone's lunch, tuna salad the next. Often, while the God Squad practiced, she sat in the back and hummed along. In the late afternoons, she walked to a massive redwood growing nearby and watched the shadows slide between the trees.

One evening, sitting around after dinner in the living room, Maya passed her a joint. Lollie held it between her thumb and first finger and breathed in deeply, as she'd seen the others do. She gagged from the heat of the smoke, and, with a small gasp, exhaled most of it. When the joint came to her again, she inhaled more cautiously. When she finally exhaled, no more than a wisp of smoke was visible. Joints continued to circulate around the room; she took small tokes off each.

Settled deep into a huge floor cushion, she heard people speaking. She heard the voices as if they were musical instruments. For years, when her parents quarreled, she would strip their words of meaning. The bass fiddle was her father. Soon the oboe of her mother's voice would join in. As she became angry, it would become a badly tuned violin. Her father's counterpoint sounded like a strident tenor saxophone. She found a perverse comfort in themes of these musical quarrels, often recognizing the whole composition from a single leitmotif. The marijuana made it effortless to turn voices into tones, almost automatically. It startled her when, out of the soft woodwinds in the living room, she heard words addressed to her.

"Hi. I'm Ed."

Lollie Anne pivoted slowly so that the sounds she heard flowed evenly over each ear. A boy's face wavered, then steadied. There was a faint glow around his eyes. Her gut tightened. Yes, she thought, his name is Ed!

Ed. Edward. Eddie. Ward. A ward of whom? Award to Ed. Ed-the-bed. Yes. Would I bed Ed? Would I wed Ed? Would Ed-the-bed want to be wed or instead be led to—? She blinked. A word left Ed's mouth and floated across the room. She let it waft by her. She saw it shatter against the door frame, the bits floating down like dandelion wishes. Their eyes met.

She willed a smile. One muscle after another tensed or relaxed until the smile appeared. Then she chose a word with care, forming it with her tongue and mouth, carefully molding the cloud of moist warm air behind her teeth. "Ah," she said. She felt more comfortable at that moment than she could remember. It was not only the place and the people, but something within herself that told her she was all right, exactly as she was and however she would be in the future.

Across the room Ed looked tiny, a three-inch-high elf. Moving toward her, he grew larger. Time slowed when he lifted his foot and sped up when his foot came down. As he came nearer her mind filled with him as music fills a concert hall. Their shadows overlapped. He slid down to the floor beside her and touched her hand.

Her awareness flowed into that hand. Her energy began to blend with his. At first, she knew where his hand ended and hers began. Then their hands melted together. She felt a rush of happy tears in her hand. His hand held her tears as if they were pearls.

They didn't speak much, but it seemed to Lollie Anne as if they had been friends a long time. She didn't find it necessary to speak her thoughts; he seemed to know them. From time to time he'd laugh, a gentle laugh that made her giggle as well. She didn't let go of his hand.

Later, they made love. It was her first time, yet her body seemed to know what to do. He was inside her for a short time and then, for him, it seemed to be over. It was neither as painful as she'd feared nor as pleasurable as she'd hoped. Ed had been gentle, but soon afterward he went to sleep. Lollie Anne stayed awake for hours, watching him, waiting to see if she was in love. She became tired and, eventually, reluctantly, admitted she was bored. Finally she slept.

Two days later Ed announced he was leaving. "San Diego," he said. He gave her the address of a friend there. "He'll probably know where to find me."

That afternoon, feeling sorry for herself, she walked past the redwood trees far up into the canyon. Finding a soft place, she lay down between two rocks and napped. When she awoke, a large wood spider was starting a web directly over her. It swung out from a rock edge and fixed one thread to another, then inched back along the thread, stopping several times to spin cross-braces. Then it swung across again and laid another rib. Lollie Anne watched it move to the first thread, making each new segment an exact match of the one before. As it worked, the spider adjusted each thread, pulling it taut. As the web neared completion, the spider worked more quickly. When tie-lines were in place all the way around, it filled in the center, matching each new thread to one across the way.

Entranced and respectful, Lollie Anne slid out from under the web so carefully that the spider never stopped working.

"But why?" Maya asked. "Shadow's become part of our family."

"Her destiny's not with you yet." The older woman's tone was sharp, as if she were saying something that should be obvious.

"But she's barely out of the nest."

"Let her wings unfold."

"She's so young."

"Old enough to run away from home," the woman said with a sniff. "Almost eighteen. In China, she would be carrying her third child."

"She is not Chinese and she is still a little girl," Maya insisted. "She needs protection."

"Since you seem to know her destiny, perhaps you know enough to run everyone else's life as well." The teacher was standing now, as if she was about to bow to Maya.

"I don't know, but that's how I feel."

"She is unready, but not unable," the older woman said firmly, terminating the discussion.

The other band members looked at one another. "We can't just push her out," the drummer said. "She has no money and knows nobody but us," the guitarist added.

"Christ's body has a thousand arms. Rootless, she came to you. You took her in. Pass her on."

They looked at each other, then back to the teacher. One by one, they nodded their willingness to do as she'd asked. The teacher did not allow her face to register disappointment at their all too swift acquiescence. "We'll start with the new arrangement of 'Earth Love,'" she said.++

They picked up their instruments and settled themselves on the redwood deck. The morning fog had lifted from the squat oaks and laurels but still clung to the tops of the cluster of pines towering above the house. By the time they finished the second run-through, the deck was in sunlight.

"It needs a stronger vocal line," the teacher said. "Trevor, come in on the chorus!"

"My voice—"

"I'm aware of its limitations. Now again, from the top. Take each chorus twice."

At the end of the practice session, they sat in meditation. As they became quiet they became aware of the light on their faces, heard the scuffling noises of squirrels running from limb to limb, and inhaled the pungent scent of California laurel. Afterward, the teacher allowed questions.

"May we tell Shadow we came to you for advice?" the drummer asked.

"Is that her name?"

"Well, she kinda follows us around." The drummer looked at the teacher, then up into the trees. "She likes it."

The teacher waited until they were attentive again. "Telling others you have a teacher, or worse, a 'guru,' distorts the teaching. It leads to vanity and avoids responsibility."

"But don't you have a teacher?" Maya asked.

"There was a woman," the teacher replied, "who came up to a famous geologist at the end of his lecture on the causes and effects of the tides. 'Earth is not rolling loose in space, as you have described,' she said, 'but sits squarely on a platform that rests on the back of an eagle that stands on a giant turtle.' The scientist, amused, asked her what this turtle stood on. The woman's eyes sparkled. 'Oh, sir, I'm no fool! It's turtles all the way down.'"

Maya wrinkled her nose. "I don't get it."

"It's teachers all the way down." She rose and bowed low to them. "Your friend may stay with you another two days. Then she goes to San

Francisco. You have friends there. Consider which of them will serve her best."

Undisturbed, the spider lived another six weeks. Her web caught a number of deer flies and two oak moths. Eventually she mated. Soon afterward she ate her mate, laid her eggs and left her web to die. By the time another generation of spiders were staking out web sites, Lollie Anne had long forgotten what she had seen being created.

CHAPTER 6

One too many mornings

I take goodness for granted.
I expect everybody to be good.

Henry Miller to Anaïs Nin

HEY GIRLY-GIRL, my mitts look like rough-cut timber 'cause I'm a carpenter," Thomas said. His conga drum's head faced away from Shadow so that all she saw was its black shiny barrel. She blushed and looked down at her bare feet. Since the God Squad left her at the Clayton house, Thomas had been by twice. He'd smoke dope, drink wine, drum for a few hours, hug everyone and leave.

She sat close enough to him to feel the drumbeats against her body. Once, he reached over and stroked her cheek with the back of his hand. Then he began to play very softly, just to her, no louder than raindrops sounding on a thin roof.

She was elated when he invited her to a party that weekend. Eddie and Moonflower were going. Sweeps told her that the house was a trip and a half. Thomas said he'd pick her up on his way out of the city. "You can have dinner with me and my wife before anyone else shows up."

Saturday afternoon they drove over the Golden Gate, past Mill Valley and Tiburon, took an exit under the freeway and headed up into the hills. Soon Thomas turned onto a dirt road lined with soaring pine trees and up an even smaller road that twisted across the top of a narrow ridge. Thomas banked sharply from one side to the other to avoid the many uneven ridges and holes in the road. Shadow breathed deeply to let Thomas see that his driving scared her.

The floor and ceiling of Thomas' house was a polished patchwork of odd-length boards. "The ends of jobs," he said, as he watched her look around admiringly.

"Did you build it?" Shadow asked.

"Don't I wish. Don't have the skills or the patience."

Shadow sat down on a padded window seat. She swung her legs back and forth and clapped her hands with pleasure. Thomas' wife, Jessica, called out a hello from the kitchen.

When Jessica emerged, Shadow saw she was a tiny woman with long, smooth auburn hair. She wore no makeup. It looked as if she wasn't wearing underwear either, just a dress that revealed her small frame. Jessica asked Shadow where she was from.

"I'm a runaway."

"Good for you," Jessica said, and gave her neck a little kiss.

Shadow beamed. If she had folks like them, she'd never leave home.

Through the windows, she saw fog filling the canyon in waves. The light outside faded to brownish-gray. She began to shiver. Jessica found her a huge green sweater. After she put it on Jessica said, "You look like the flower in the center of a beautiful plant."

"Positively pluckable," Thomas said.

They ate at a table in the kitchen. Thomas served Shadow a drink in a tall glass with mint leaves hanging on the lip.

"What is it?" she asked, pointing exactly the way her mother had said was rude.

"Perfect for the end of a day," Thomas said, pouring out two more.

Shadow drank hers before she'd finished her fruit salad. She felt giggly. "Is there much liquor in it?"

"More than your mom would serve you," Jessica answered.

"You sure are more fun than they are."

Thomas and Jessica looked at each other. All three of them laughed.

Shadow had licked her ice cream dish clean and was reaching over for Jessica's, when the door was thrown open. Two couples bounded in, helloing loudly. Shadow and Jessica cleaned up the remains of the dinner as guests continued to arrive. Carrying dishes out to the kitchen, Shadow stumbled a few times, but didn't drop a thing.

More people came in. Shadow waved to Moonflower as soon as she saw her, but Moonflower was talking excitedly with a black man in a red vest and gave her no more than a quick nod. Nitrous Eddie came over, but he was already too stoned for her to understand him. People set up their own drums; a few had brought other rhythm instruments. Music filled the house.

Feeling a little queasy, Shadow went outside to get away from the noise. After a few steps, she looked back. The fog was so dense that she could see nothing of the house, only the lighted rectangle of each window. When she came back in, most people were dancing to the drums, or their own private rhythms. Next to a big bowl of avocado dip and a plate of chips, a small brass tray held a semicircle of rolled joints. A few had been lit and were being passed among the guests.

Thomas was drumming hard; sweat dripped down his arms onto the drum head. Shadow found a dish towel in the kitchen and wiped him off. He blew her a kiss. She sat by his feet until a man stretched out a hand and pulled her up to dance. At first he just echoed her moves; then he danced a bass line while she danced melody. He took off his shirt. They didn't touch except when he brushed her body with his fingertips. Shadow took little sucks off the joints that passed by. Gradually the drumming took her over. She felt dizzy, light-headed and gloriously happy, sure that she loved these people. When she was holding the end of a joint too small to smoke but still burning, a man with a huge head of black curly hair and a tattoo of a cross on the back of his right hand took it from her fingers with an alligator clip. Then he ate it. She laughed so hard she almost peed.

Thomas and Jessica were dancing now. When Thomas lifted Jessica's sweater up over her head, Shadow was surprised to see she had nothing on underneath.

Shadow danced with herself. She danced the pieces of wood in the ceiling and the trees they were cut from. She danced the fog cascading down the hills. She danced the earth holding up the house. She danced gratitude for the animals whose skins stretched over the drums. She danced her body's eagerness to dance.

She didn't remember everything that happened after that. She danced with Moonflower. They fell down on a bunch of people and rolled over and over them. She remembered she'd danced lying down for a while after that. She knew she took off the green sweater.

She remembered being in Thomas' arms, gliding around the floor. Everyone else had gone. They were both naked, swaying together. His penis pressed against her. She'd pulled away, confused. Then she felt Jessica, naked as well, behind her. She hugged Shadow, kissed her cheek, licked her ear. She saw the three of them reflected in the living room windows. Thomas laughed his big soft laugh. Jessica stroked Shadow's hips; reaching around her, she cupped Shadow's breasts and kissed her back and neck. She held Shadow up as Thomas moved in and out of her. Between their two bodies, Shadow felt suspended, her feet barely touching the floor. Thomas was inside her, pushing. Jessica moved her with him. He and Jessica made noises as if they were a single person. When Thomas climaxed, Jessica seemed to as well.

Shadow felt waves of intense sensation, as if every part of her body was being caressed. Simultaneously, part of her had no feeling at all; it just watched Thomas holding her, his belly pressed against hers. She felt each of Jessica's fingers on her chest, one fingertip pressing each nipple. This was all happening, but to someone else. Then the wave would catch her and she'd lose awareness of herself. Later, lying by herself, the waves receded. Finally she slept.

CHAPTER 7

For the betterment of mankind

*Research
in the manipulation of human behavior
is considered by many authorities
in medicine and related fields
to be professionally unethical.*

CIA Inspector General
in a review of that agency's drug studies

L ANGWATER DID NOT BELIEVE in torture. Not that he found it personally repugnant; he'd simply concluded it was counterproductive. In the CIA projection room, he'd spent days watching films of people being tortured. He smoked incessantly and took copious notes. Often, he stopped the projector and walked up to the screen to look more closely at a face in pain.

His published papers argued that torture was a prepsychological methodology that went against human nature. Human beings were designed to withstand pain, and pain triggered biochemical protective mechanisms. Thus, in the application of physical torture, people's bio-chemistry underwent changes that made them better able to sustain noncooperation. Additional pain actually reinforced resistance.

Moreover, he maintained, information obtained from torture was often riddled with inconsistencies and fabrications. By the time subjects' defenses were truly destroyed, their physical state would be so deterio-rated that their memories would be genuinely impaired, as would their grasp of the relative importance of events. While in this state, people tended to retain accurate recollections of isolated details, such as the col-or of an instrument panel or the name of a hotel; however, they became progressively more unsure of simple facts, such as the number of men in a military unit or the amount and kinds of ammunition stored in a bunker. Pure abstractions, such as location coordinates or the code word for an operation, became impossible to recall.

Langwater concluded that simple physical punishment was accept-able only if the purpose was to instill fear or to release sadistic predispo-sitions in those who did the torturing. However, if one needed to extract information, or, better yet, turn resisters into collaborators, one had to see people as "mental bodies." The linkages between their values, their view of themselves, and their identification with their cause were the critical keys.

In a major address to the American Psychiatric Association, he ar-gued that if you could precipitate a process of disassociation, informa-tion, no matter how tightly held or how highly valued by the former identity, would lose its emotional valence. In other words, it wouldn't be worth the price of withholding if it had become part of a prior personal-ity configuration.

Langwater proposed that those involved in administering physical torture be retrained to help persons under their control construct new personality constellations. Sharing previously withheld information would be reframed as part of the recovery process.

Most of the psychiatric audience concluded that Langwater's ideas were by-products of a disturbed childhood, stultifying professional training and intense envy of colleagues who had more prestige. Some in the international intelligence community, however, considered his work a hallmark of growing sophistication in the mental sciences in general and mind manipulation in particular. Soon after the speech, the secret services of several countries asked Langwater to submit research proposals. He basked in their enthusiasm and zealously created a sheaf of experimental possibilities.

He considered himself a moral man and saw his suggestions for inducing psychological disorientation as more humane and enlightened than current practices. He believed his ideas could rescue individuals from what he called the "witless barbarism of physical torture."

He was so enthused by the possibilities of doing large-scale tests of his ideas that he began to use his own private psychiatric patients as subjects. Clients whose presenting symptoms were nothing more than simple situational maladjustments, unhappy relationships or problems at work began to disintegrate when Langwater treated them with drugs, isolation and his own confusion techniques. Many eventually required hospitalization. When they were in a fully controlled institutional setting, Langwater accelerated the process of disintegration. Privately circulated reports of these pilot studies convinced the Central Intelligence Agency that his ideas were worth full-scale field verification.

He was made a Senior Research Fellow—a job classification which gave him access to the Agency's higher levels as well as gratifying his need for recognition. After eighteen months of work inside the Agency, he felt ready to work with populations other than prisoners or psychiatric patients. He proposed that regular civilian and military personnel be waylaid, thus simulating what might occur in an actual conflict. One facility to further that research was established in San Francisco.

Early research with the psychedelic drug LSD-25 suggested that it created a brief but full-blown schizophrenic reaction with extensive hallucinatory side effects that included depersonalization and distortion of the body image. Langwater reasoned that these effects would be heightened if the drugs were given surreptitiously. In a real-life situation, subjects would have no idea what had caused their chaotic mental state. The resulting disorganization could be employed to extract information.

The site was found, the building prepared, the staff hired, and the research begun. Langwater contented himself with periodic trips to San Francisco to modify the protocols and review the results. He left to others the day-to-day administration, the experimental protocols, the security precautions and the cover to disguise the project and its sponsor.

On this brief trip to San Francisco, Langwater did little more than berate the staff for the paucity of their results.

"On my next visit I will personally oversee a night's work," he said. "You had all better know your business or you will be looking for jobs elsewhere."

CHAPTER 8

The stars see us spinning

"Why you should bother your head
about such damned nonsense
is more than I can grasp.
It's meaningless to me," said Bjartur.

Halldór Laxness, *Independent People*

SHADOW WOKE UP DIZZY and nauseous, her head a pincushion of pain. When she opened her eyes, she saw a small glass vase near her head, filled with fresh cornflowers. She read the note that leaned against it.

We both love you.
Had to go to work.
There's a glass of morning-after in the fridge.
We'll call someone at your house to get you home.

Two illegible signatures under it.

She staggered to the toilet and threw up. Then she crawled to the refrigerator and drank the glass of whatever it was. It tasted awful, but she kept it down. She lay naked on the kitchen floor and slept again. Later, wrapping a blanket around herself, she walked gingerly to a window seat, curled up on the cushions and looked into the deep canyon. The fog was dissipating. When it burned off, she could see the edge of the sea.

Close to noon, Sweeps showed up. Driving back, he told her that two guys had gone off the road's edge leaving the party.

"Were they hurt?" Shadow asked.

"No," Sweeps said. "The car rolled over a few times, but they were so mellow, they just bounced. When the car got hung up in the brush, they squeezed out the windows. Both walked away." Sweeps glanced at her. "You look a little gray-green. You okay?"

"I had a lot of booze," she said. She opened the window and stuck her head out. The wet air hitting her face made her feel better.

"Such a downer. You should have smoked dope."

"I did."

Sweeps was quiet. She couldn't tell him about the sex with Thomas and Jessica. She couldn't tell anyone. As they drove on in silence, she remembered, right at the end, she'd reached out and pulled Thomas even closer. She felt sick again, and ashamed. She stuck her head all the way out the car window and, like a dog, turned her face into the wind. She hoped Sweeps wouldn't see her tears.

After leaving Shadow at the house to finish sleeping it off, Sweeps felt relieved to be back on his own. On Sundays he preferred to cruise the trash cans in Golden Gate Park just before dark. The cans were full then. They would not be emptied until morning. On other days, park personnel appeared at dusk, emptying everything. Keeping a watch out for them took much of the pleasure out of sifting, sorting and deciding.

Before starting on the cans, he'd crisscrossed the paths and lawns on the Panhandle and near the bandstand. He found two sweaters, both far too small for his long arms. He turned up a child's purse with a dollar, a nickel and three pennies, most of a pack of playing cards from the Sands in Las Vegas, two earrings—one possibly silver—and enough packaged food to last several days.

He was convinced that he was a whirling central sun of exceptionalness. Never before had anyone, head down, digging deep into a trash can in Golden Gate Park, possessed so much literary erudition pasted onto the folds of his cerebrum. His hands turned over layers of trash and opened lunch bags covered with sticky ice cream and cigarette ash while his mind echoed with passages and images from writers he loved.

"There will never be any more perfection than there is now,

Nor any more heaven or hell than is now!"

Whitman, he knew, would have understood this moment, Whitman who loved everything and anything, whose sexual tastes for rough trade he'd transmuted into blissed-out poems about everyman.

"The god of the heart—for all that he is a god, he goes many crooked ways. Goes out adventuring. The wild thing he is. One day rolling in a bed of roses and licking his lips, next day with a thorn in his foot." Knut Hamsun knew so much about poverty that he never blamed any of his characters for it.

Sweeps found an orange. He judged it worth saving and laid it carefully on the bench nearby. His mind flashed to Count Rostov's multi-course, multiwine dinner party in *War and Peace*. A servant stood behind each guest pouring wine into, ah. . . so many crystal glasses. He imagined his orange on a solid silver serving dish, its reflective surface exaggerating its color. No, Tolstoy was too effete for him today. He was closer to the hard-edged times of Dostoevsky's people. He recalled Razumihin saying, "Though all my friends there are drunk, yet they are all honest, and though we do talk a lot of trash, and I do too, yet we shall talk our way to the truth at last, for we are on the right path." What would Dostoevsky have written had he been in San Francisco now?

Sweeps looked around, half expecting to see a ragged Russian student, and was momentarily unnerved by a diverse group of onlookers arrayed in a semicircle around him. A crowd of seagulls watched, practically standing under his feet; two ravens stood behind them and five gray squirrels fidgeted a few feet away. He ripped up the remains of a soggy jelly sandwich and threw the bits between the birds and the squirrels, setting off a scramble. Those who seized a piece fled the circle, racing to keep ahead of those trying to tear it from them.

"There are no words for such kindheartedness toward a stranger. And don't apologize, it's the kindness of the heart that matters, not the coffee or the chicory." Laxness' failed poet, in World Light. Sweeps wished he could think these jewels without his tight-ass mind adding footnotes. Better than Frank's raw oysters, though.

He spent ten more minutes distributing food scraps to his unruly flock, which shrank and then expanded in brief feeding frenzies. Satisfied, he put everything he wanted to keep into a multicolored shopping bag from Raponzi's of Rome which had held an almost empty bottle of 1963 Chateau Neuf du Pape. Scattering the animals with a wave of the bag, he headed up the park toward Clayton Street.

He saw himself as a gleaner for the Age of Aquarius, wanting little, wasting less. Sweeps pulled up the collar of his jacket; the frayed edges rubbed pleasantly against his cheek and the cold tip of the zipper touched his chin.

Images of German children after World War II sifting through the garbage in front of exploded buildings floated into his mind. The children turned and held out their hands, small as squirrels, their faces like tiny skulls. A burly young man his own age passed by. He was wearing combat boots. Looked a little like Lew Wallins, who had gone over to Vietnam early on, before Sweeps even had any clear idea where the place was. Lew hadn't even been a soldier, just an interpreter working for the U.S. military "advisers." He'd been killed before the government had begun to trump up their patriotic fantasies to bolster a failed colonialist regime. Sweeps felt for his wallet; in it was his draft card—4-F.

How good it had been to flunk something! Hadn't been easy to make 4-F, physically unfit to be bombed, shot at or stabbed—unable to kill for the greater glory of God, flag and country.

Only after his friend Randy, a graduate student in high-energy physics, got 4-F did Sweeps consider it. Randy's counselor sent a letter to the draft board that described Randy as a repressed faggot who'd pop under pressure and would try to kiss every man in his squad. "I wrote it," Randy told him. "He just signed it. My first publication."

No matter how trivial and worthless graduate school seemed, it looked better than the military and way ahead of Vietnam. Sweeps hated the war not only because it was wrong, but also because he was terrified that if he were in it, he might be wounded, tortured or killed.

From a draft resisters' group on campus, he heard about a fitness instructor at the Palo Alto YMCA who could help a person flunk the physical. Sweeps met him on a chill, cloudy February afternoon outside the Y.

The instructor was shorter than Sweeps, with a barrel chest, short, muscled arms and a crew cut. He looked Sweeps over. "I'll help you," he said in a soft Southern drawl.

"How?" Sweeps asked.

"I can teach you yoga postures that'll raise your blood pressure and keep it up through your physical. Take some work, though. You up for it, boy?"

"Is it safe?"

"A whole lot safer than having your ass shot off."

"Why are you doing this for me?" Sweeps asked, after the silence between them had gone on too long.

"Why's a dumb jock helping a college coward fade the draft?" The instructor looked right through Sweeps. "I was an NCO in Korea—with the Wolfhounds. We were the toughest. The best!" His upper body tensed. "I've killed a lot of little yellow people. Got a box of medals and ribbons."

Gray sheets of cloud moved slowly above them. "One night I was leading my patrol up a hill—three of us. Had to use my forty-five to keep the other two guys going. While I covered our tails, those two turned a corner. A mortar shell took their heads off." He lit a cigarette. "One of those guys had been to college."

"Can I pay you?"

"Sure, mister. Put in stateside time against the war and we'll be square."

"You got a deal."

"How many push-ups can you do?"

Sweeps mentally doubled his all-time best. "Eight."

"Pull-ups?"

Sweeps paused. "Two," he answered truthfully.

"You might not need my help to get 4-F."

"Not my fault I was always picked last in gym."

"Bullshit, buddy. Everything is everyone's fault. But who the fuck cares? Come back tomorrow at six-thirty. Sit here till I show up."

Over the next few weeks, Sweeps learned to stand on his head, to contract his anus and clench his neck muscles while keeping his facial muscles relaxed. He began to almost enjoy push-ups. Push-ups for peace, he called them—but only to himself.

The pimply med tech took his blood pressure, then took it again. He shook his head as he wrote something on the chart. "Any blood pressure problems in your family?"

"No, sir. Well, wait. That's not strictly true. One uncle—my dad's brother had it. He died of something else though, I think. My mom's parents couldn't eat salty food. Said it was blood pressure." Sitting naked on the wooden bench, Sweeps stared at the wall over the man's shoulder, his fear helping maintain the tension throughout his body.

"Well, you've got problems, buddy. You're not going into this man's army. You got the blood pressure of a guy fifty pounds heavier and thirty years older."

Sweeps' jaw relaxed a little. "No shit."

The tech didn't hide his contempt. "I took it twice. Get dressed and pick up your papers."

"Isn't there medicine I can take to lower it? Could I come back and get another test?"

The med tech looked down at him. "Nobody fakes his way into this army. You think we want you crapping out under fire? If I say you're out, you're out. For life, mister."

The way he said "mister" filled Sweeps with joy; the subtext was explicit—defective, weakling, dog shit! Sweeps suppressed an urge to pump the other man's hand and thank him.

Exhibiting what he hoped looked like sullen disappointment, he was mustered out of the examining room and out of the army. He could still be called, he was told, until he was twenty-six. "If the Commies come over here, mister, your 4-F card is toilet paper. You got that?" The sergeant blew cigarette smoke in his face.

Sweeps turned his face away and made a tiny chirping sound to suppress a cough. "Yes... sir." He stood up straight, but not straight enough to evoke the slightest respect. As he walked out, he heard someone say, "Key rryst—high blood pressure! Why don't these college dicks get in shape?"

"So sorry, most honorable officer jerk-off. So very sorry! Not able join you lovely army," Sweeps murmured. He walked slowly, shoulders drooping, until he was around the corner, when he broke into a joyful high-stepping run.

CHAPTER 9

Father Finnbar O'Malley

*A hippie is someone who
dresses like Tarzan,
has hair like Jane
and smells like Cheetah.*

California Governor Ronald Reagan

FATHER FINNBAR O'MALLEY was standing in the entrance of the Church of St. John as Sweeps folded the two sweaters and laid them on the steps. Finnbar cleared his throat loudly. Sweeps looked up. "For the poor box." He pointed to the sweaters. "I've used it myself. Thought I'd put a little back in the stream."

"Why don't you hand them to me. I'll make sure they'll make some folks grateful." They smiled at one another. "Nice to have caring people in my parish."

"I'm no Catholic, Father. This neighborhood takes care of its own."

"Hope you're right." Finnbar held the sweaters to his chest. "I'm new here."

"A lot of us are turned on to God, but honestly, Father, not too many are finding him in the churches."

"Then I'll have to get out more."

Sweeps smiled. "You've got the right idea." He gestured around him. "Lots of saints in the neighborhood. Nitrous Eddie says this is holy ground."

Finnbar put out his hand. "My name is Finnbar O'Malley. Yours?"

"Call me Sweeps."

Finnbar looks puzzled.

"It's a street name. The way people would get named Smith or Spencer or Miller."

"Spencer?"

"It's derived from the servant who was the dis-spencer. Get it?"

Finnbar came down the steps and stood next to Sweeps. "Some people call me Father Finn."

"After the hero Finn MacCool?"

Finnbar beamed. "Don't I wish I were from the stock of Fionn mac Cumhail. Not many people are as knowledgeable as you. My family was wanting a girl. My name's the male version of Finnabair."

When Sweeps displayed no sign of recognition, Finn explained, "The Irish Guinevere."

"Oh, that's cool," Sweeps said, stepping away. He retreated to the sidewalk. "Hey, Finnbar, nice to meet you. See you 'round."

Whiffs of wet night fog eased around the corner. Someone on a balcony across the street was playing a guitar and singing Dylan's version of "Don't Think Twice, It's All Right." Sweeps zipped his jacket up to his chin and repeated to himself, It's all right, it's all right. Then, without looking up again at the priest, he started down Haight Street. Finnbar, still wondering if he'd been rejected, watched Sweeps walk a full block before admitting he was gone. He headed back up the steps.

Finnbar O'Malley was part of a large extended Boston Irish family that included more than a few priests and nuns in each generation. He was too young and too short to command respect, and he weighed a little too much to be called trim. His hair, already sparse in front, made him seem slighter but not older than his twenty-four years. His blue eyes did not sparkle, and his forehead already displayed a few lines above a small blunt nose. He had been out of seminary less than two years, working with teenage groups in Roxbury, when he was reassigned to San Francisco.

In seminary, he had envied Christ's not having to study the New Testament. When he'd confessed his envy, he'd been laughed at, even in the confessional.

The street-smart kids he worked with in Roxbury on a daily basis were no different from the ones who'd frightened him during high school. The fact that he was no longer in competition with them for grades or girls made him feel almost secure. Contrary to the prevailing attitude, he even went to bat for them against a juvenile justice system that seemed perversely eager to affix criminal records on them for every minor infraction. He worried about their health and sometimes packed food parcels for them to take home for out-of-work parents.

Eric the Red, the gang leader whose territory included Finnbar's clubhouse, said, "Fadder, you're all right—for a priest. If anyone gives you shit, tell me. I'll break their head." It gave Finnbar a great deal of pride to be accepted—pride that would have been deflated had he known that Eric referred to him privately as "the eenie weenie priest."

In the spirit of his vocation, he accepted his reassignment with regret, but he didn't object. At their last meeting, Eric punched him hard on his upper arm. "Just so you don't forget me, Fadder. Tell God I'm your friend!"

Assigned to the Youth Guidance Program of the Diocese of San Francisco, he replaced Father Daniel, a much older priest. "Not a day too soon," Father Daniel said at their first meeting. As he spoke, his upper lip twitched and his red nose, already a caricature of a priest's beak, went several shades redder. "My people come from out East," he said, as if it were a reason. The truth was that Father Daniel preferred older people for their deference to his position and opinions. He had, in fact, pleaded to be allowed to relocate. "The youth of this parish," he'd said with understated accuracy, "no longer trust me."

The Church of St. John, which had as its jurisdiction most of the Haight-Ashbury neighborhood, housed Father O'Malley in a room facing an alley, a mere slot that allowed him barely enough space to sleep and pray. While depressed by it, he did not complain.

By the end of his first week, Finnbar had walked in every part of the neighborhood. On three separate occasions, young men dressed as if going to costume parties offered to sell him LSD. A pretty dark-haired girl, not more than thirteen, who called herself Sunlight, gently asked him for spare change. When he offered to take her to the church for a good meal, she declined. "I live with my parents in San Mateo, Father. I don't need charity."

"Then why—?" he asked.

"To go to the Fillmore. You should come. It's fantastic."

Another girl gave him a marijuana cigarette and told him to smoke it before mass. "Suck a little God in—blow your mind, padre!" Unwilling to throw it away, he kept it hidden in a rolled Kleenex in the back of his desk drawer.

Twice, young girls asked him to come up to their pads. He was too embarrassed to ask why. Another girl, a head taller than he was, wearing red cowboy boots and a halter top, asked, "Will you fuck me in the church?" Involuntarily, he jerked back. She looked into his eyes. "I've always wanted that. I just haven't found the right priest." Before he could collect his thoughts, she'd turned away.

He set the sweaters on the edge of his small desk. He took out a piece of paper, wound it into his tiny Olivetti portable and began to type.

```
                                        October 19, 1966
Dear Mom,

    I know I'm still in the good old U.S. of A. but,
still, after being here only a week, it is as if I've
```

been resettled in a foreign country. These people
have no money, but they don't behave like the poor.
Only a few have jobs; yet they survive — without wel-
fare. Their ideas and manners are nothing like the
Irish, Italian, or even the Negro families of
greater Roxbury (that right now I miss very much).

There are no families here, in fact, or so it
seems. On the streets and in the stores I meet only
young people. A few older ones run small businesses,
but it is as if they have been bused in. At night
they vanish, leaving behind a society of post-pubes-
cent boys and girls whose emotional ties to their
blood relatives are as thin as mouse hair.

No one seems to be from here; they are all immigrants without anyone to guide them or protect them.
But, then again, you could say that of me too. I feel
rootless too. When I ask after their people they
tell me they're somewhere else—Ohio, Iowa, Fairfax
(wherever that is), even "the dark side of the
moon."

Today, a boy said to me, "Man, my parents are so
far out of it, being dead would make them hipper."
Another, clearly hungry, but not begging, said, "My
Dad is 10,000 years away from anyplace real. And my
Mom? Who ever heard from her?" A young girl yelled at
me, "Parents? Never heard of them. Anything like
cops?" She actually spit on the street in front of
me.

They appear to violate every social belief that
I've learned to value. But Mom, it's very strange:
in spite of their dirt, their evident promiscuity,
their drug use, and their stinging disrespect for

almost anything and anyone, there's a saintly quality about many of them.

He didn't mention that yesterday a girl with beautiful gray-green eyes
and dreamy, innocent speech had propositioned him. When she touched
him—only the slightest brush along the back of his hand—he wished
he'd said yes.

They hold hands a lot, these street people, and
hug one another, like early Christians. They take
care of one another, take in the homeless ones, and
share their food (which often isn't much) if a
stranger appears.
    It's as if a collection of crazed antisocial va-
grants have covertly found Christ.

Finnbar found himself not knowing what people meant when they
spoke to him and even less when they spoke to each other. He was desperately lonely and began attending mass more and more often, just to
be with human beings whose behavior he understood. He clung to mass
as if it were the last lighted candle in a sea of benevolent but terrifying
darkness.

    He prayed to discover ways to reach these young souls, but more of-
ten he simply prayed to be less lonely. Sometimes, when he prayed, he'd
touch the place where Eric had bruised him as someone else might hold
a rosary.

PART II

CHAPTER 10

No better job

It has so happened, in all ages of the world,
that some have labored,
and others have, without labor,
enjoyed a large proportion of the fruits.
This is wrong and should not continue.

Abraham Lincoln

ALPHIE, YOUR AUNT ROUND HEELS is on the social pages again. Very la-de-da, if you ask me." His mother's voice jabbed at Bear. "Still looks like an old whore—even after the face-lift."

He held the receiver farther from his ear.

"I mean really, my own sister! Not even a Christmas card. I still send her one every year."

"Yes, Momma, you do," Bear said evenly. At least she'd stopped asking what he was doing. Outraged as his mother was at her own sister's life, she'd be apoplectic if she knew—not only about this job, but about other projects he'd done for the Agency. She still worried that he was nothing more than a midlevel government drudge.

"Have to go, Momma. Weather here is gloomy and cold, like always. Don't believe them about California. New Orleans has it all over this place."

"Stop trying to make me feel good about this crappy apartment. I can always tell when you fib. Damn air conditioner drips wet rust— when it works!"

Bear rapped loudly on his desk with his knuckles. "Yeah, Momma, just kidding. This is a nice place." He rapped again. "Hold on a minute!" he shouted to his empty office. "I'm coming! Hold the damn horses." He spoke in a forced whisper into the phone. "Got to go, Momma. Eat right, walk light, sleep tight. Bye." Putting the phone down, he leaned back in his chair, took out a crumpled handkerchief and wiped tiny beads of sweat from his forehead.

Until recently, managing a taxpayer-supported whorehouse had given him a perverse pleasure unmatched by any other government job. But not today. He'd just read a classified report leaked to him by a friend that described Langwater as "an innovative but emotionally immature researcher." Langwater's recent tantrums, the report said, had almost caused the whole project to be terminated.

Bear looked over the accounts for the last quarter. He'd just about got things running smoothly. Another six months. Hell, they might even turn a profit.

Tucked away in his own top-secret clearance file were facts he'd thought were well hidden but that had surfaced when the CIA looked for someone to run this experimental station. During college, Bear had done the record-keeping and banking for his Aunt Suzanne's whorehouse in Hattiesburg, Mississippi.

He walked down the hall and dropped the sheets on his assistant's desk. "Lou, look at the items I've marked. It's the usual petty stuff. Tell Madame we'll can her if she tries to fuck us over again."

Lou looked up over his glasses. "Are you serious?"

"Hell, no. I just want to hold her stealing to a reasonable rate, so we don't get questions. Tell her I'm ready to explode, but you'll try to defuse me. Tell her to keep her greed under control."

"Can do. Will do," Lou said. "Anything from Washington?"

"Nothing we can do anything about. They've closed down about sixty projects. All over the country."

Lou let out a surprised whistle.

"Whenever another ten thousand kids turn on, the agencies clamp down—somewhere else. A full-blown case of pushing your head deep in the sand so you can't see someone shooting at your ass."

Lou picked up the papers. "I'll do what I can to keep our end up." When Bear didn't seem to hear the joke, Lou's self-congratulatory smile faded.

Lou was an efficient administrator, keeping each group in the project ignorant of the others in certain critical ways and still gaining everyone's cooperation. It was important that the clients think this house was a bit better than some others. Lou made sure that the liquor flowed freely and the girls' prices stayed low. To maintain an upscale tone in a seedy location, the girls were under strict orders not to roll the johns, no matter how drugged or drunk they became. The girls, in turn, supplemented their normal pay by artfully embezzling every dime they could from the research side. For many of them, the house had become a real home. Even on evenings when experiments were run, they complained only among themselves.

The madame took more than her agreed upon share of the extra pay and padded her books. She regularly thanked a yellowing plastic statue of Saint Claire that sat beside her dresser mirror for her luck.

The college students—Brad, Angelo and the others listed on the duty roster as research assistants—knew about the petty thievery. Unlike the madame and the girls, they had some idea of the actual purpose of the research, but they didn't realize they were dupes brought in to maintain another layer of cover for the operation. Among themselves, they congratulated each other on seeing both sides of life at an early age.

Among other chores, the students compiled and copied the data sheets and wrote up monthly summaries. They also kept hot food available for the staff on data-collection nights. Occasionally they even served as runners, taking johns back to their pickup points. To fill their hours, they were given useless tasks, including writing reports to the CIA front foundations that sent their monthly stipends. Thus the students, lightly burdened and overpaid, were bought into silence without being asked.

Angelo and Brad and the other students stayed out of the whorehouse, except when the observers, seated behind one-way glass with clipboards and stopwatches, rated the interactions of experimental and control subjects on "Verbal clarity," "Level of emotional affect," "Duration of sexual contact," "Autobiographical statements," and other items in the protocols.

Those who knew the real purpose of the research and the real employer doubted that the data would ever be used or even useful. Lou said one afternoon over a beer, "This secret protects itself! Who do I know— who do you guys know—who'd believe we're getting paid to watch people fuck while their brains fall out?"

As Bear knew it would, the clipping about Aunt Suzanne came in the mail. The photograph showed her standing with several other women near a huge vase of flowers. The caption identified them as hostesses for a benefit for the Oxner Eye Clinic. "One of the major charitable events of the season" was the caption. Bear admired his aunt. She'd played the cards she'd been dealt better than anyone would have predicted.

The Hattiesburg police chief had become such a friend of Suzanne's that her house paid no protection money in its final years. When he was promoted to Chief of Security of the Port of New Orleans, he scandalized the locals by marrying her. The couple bought a rundown mansion on the edge of a fashionable quarter of New Orleans. From there, his aunt began her climb up the social ladder, a task at which she became increasingly proficient. In five years, she'd become too prominent to associate with any of her relatives, including her sister or Bear.

Bear stared at the photograph. Some days he wished he could call Suzanne for advice. He crumpled up the clipping and tossed it into the wastebasket.

CHAPTER 11

Angelo and Shadow

The two plum trees:
One blooms early.
The other later.

Buson

THE TRIP SHOP
outfitters for inner travellers.

NGELO READ THE SIGN TWICE. He pushed the door open, feeling as shy as when he'd gone into a drugstore to buy condoms. Madras cloths covered one wall. A polished brass cash register sat on a small desk. In a glass case, packages of cigarette papers encircled a tray of rings. Books and records mingled haphazardly along one wall and boxes of merchandise on shelves behind the cash register reached almost to the rafters. A poster tacked to the ceiling displayed a hand made of an American flag, the third finger extending straight up. "FUCK WAR!" was printed below it.

Bewildered, Angelo hesitated. As he held on to the door frame, a voice came from the back of the shop. "See what you want?"

"Um, no."

"Can I help?" Shadow materialized in front of him, her hair pinned up, wearing a thin India-print table throw like a sari.

"Uh, do you have incense?"

"Any special kind?"

Her smile distracted him. "I don't know much about incense."

"What kind of holder do you have?"

"Holder?"

"Do you want a holder?"

He shifted his weight from one foot to the other. "Do I need one?"

She stepped behind the counter. "With stick incense, you can put it in a little flowerpot or even a glass. Other kinds need a holder."

How should he know? Why wasn't Brad doing this? Incense had been his idea.

Shadow glided across the room, smoothly rose up on her toes and pulled down a cardboard box from a shelf far above her head. From it, she brought out two incense packets wrapped in slightly torn, colorful and wrinkled paper. "I like sandalwood, but jasmine is nice, too," she said, holding one in each hand. "Smell them."

He did. "The sandalwood smells less like perfume," he said.

"I like it best." She made a little cooing noise.

He grinned in relief.

"Do you want a holder?"

"I can use a glass."

"Oh, good."

"Do you think I should buy a holder?" He was feeling uncertain again.

"Not especially. What if you bought one and didn't need it? Bad karma for me." She glanced up at him playfully, then held up the sandalwood. "One package enough?"

He nodded.

Back outside, he looked through the window and saw her prancing

across the room, the incense box held close to her breasts. She pushed it
back onto the shelf with a little hop.

When he came back several days later she remembered him, not so
much by the way he looked, but by the way he hesitated just inside the
shop. He reminded her of a child embarrassed to ask where the toilet is.
"I shortchanged you the other day. I ran after you but you'd disappeared.
I hope you weren't mad."

He shook his head.

"I taped it to the cash register so I'd remember." She took the dime
off the cash drawer, put it into his hand and gently closed his fingers over
it.

"You d-d-didn't have to," he stammered.

"Yes, I did."

Embarrassed by the exchange, Angelo turned away. Inside a display
case, he saw stacks of small transparent boxes beside an earring tray and
some pins made with feathers and colored yarns. Something on the lid
of each box refracted the light into rainbows. "Can I see those?"

"The case opens," she said, and continued to straighten a pile of
scarves.

"It's not locked?"

"We don't lock anything." She walked over and opened the case.
"Sometimes people take stuff, but usually they come back. Pay us later.
Antonio, he's one of the owners, says it all balances out."

The keys in his pocket dug into his leg; he hoped they didn't show.
Bear locked everything—even the john.

Angelo took a plastic box out of the case, clicked it open and picked
out a square piece of flat plastic as large as a quarter and patterned with
smaller squares. Each square reflected a rainbow that rotated as he
moved it. In the box were other pieces: a smaller square, an oval, one
shaped like an eye, several with four tiny circles. Each reflected rainbows.

The bottom one was a large perfect disc. Grooved like a phonograph record, its lines were tiny, almost invisible. He turned the box over looking for more information, but there was only a price tag.

"Pretty, huh?" She was standing beside him.

He nodded. "What are they?"

"Diffraction gratings."

He picked up the scattered pieces, tamped them together and tried to fit them back into the box. She reached out, took the box, carefully turned each one, matched the edges, slipped them back into the box and snapped it shut.

He winced at his clumsiness, for not knowing what diffraction gratings were, and for not counting his change. But none of it seemed to matter to her.

"What do people do with them?" he asked.

"Whatever they want."

"Any hints?"

"Some people wear them over their third eye. I think it's there," she said, pointing to a spot above the bridge of her nose.

Avoiding her gaze, he turned the box over as if checking the price, then reached into his back pocket for his wallet.

"Just what I've been looking for," he said and handed her a dollar bill. What he wanted to say was, "Just what my third eye's been craving," but he didn't want to sound stupid.

She held his dollar and looked at him, her dark eyes focused on his own. She rubbed the bill between her fingers. "Do you want to pay the sales tax? It's okay if you don't."

"Sure." Jesus, she probably thought he was a full-scale mental defective. "Here, take it out of my lucky dime."

Stuffing his change into a pocket, he hurried out. As he walked down the street, he squeezed the plastic box without noticing until his palm hurt, trying to remember if her eyebrows had lifted with every dumb thing he'd done.

Twice that week he saw her on the street. The second time, she was wearing the Indian print as a skirt and strolling arm in arm with another girl. He followed them until they turned the corner. Then he walked on, averting his face in case she looked back.

CHAPTER 12

Easy

Let me have war, say I;
it exceeds peace
as far as day does night.

Shakespeare, *Coriolanus*, act IV, scene 5

HEY THERE, LITTLE LADY! You don't look happy, not at all."

Shadow squinted into the sun at the man who called to her. He was balanced on an old wooden fruit ladder, plucking apples and dropping them rapidly into a cloth bucket. She couldn't see his face—only a reddish beard and large nostrils. "I'm doing as good a job as anyone."

"I wasn't talking about your apples," he said cheerfully. "It's your attitude."

Her metal bucket felt heavy. Her arms were scratched and her sweat made the scratches sting. Her back hurt. And now she was getting a bum rap for her attitude. "What do folks call you?" he asked.

"Shadow."

"That's cool."

"How about you?"

"Easy. Like water rolling down a rock." He leaped down and landed in a half-crouch at her feet. The tendons in his neck and arms were visible through his light tan. Easy was small and wiry, not much taller than she was. His arms were long for his body, and his nose seemed too flat for his face. As he stood eye to eye with her, his full beard and long hair completely framed his face. "Take a rest!" he said. Without another word, he emptied his bucket into hers and climbed back up the ladder.

Moonflower was at the other end of the orchard, sitting on the ground with two of the Diggers. Shadow held her bucket in both hands. It bumped against her thighs as she walked. Moonflower, who had dragged her into this free-apples thing, wasn't even working. She stalked across the orchard, passing other pickers, to the edge of the driveway. There she emptied the bucket of small, deformed apples into a wooden crate already half-filled.

Back at the tree, Easy was humming, his hands moving deftly. "That was nice," she called up. "Made people think I was busting my tail."

"Good."

"You know," she said, "every one of those apples is like a veteran. Like they were in a war with—with bugs and everything. We're picking heroes, survivors."

"Don't be a little jerk," he said angrily. "We're killing them. How does that grab you?"

"I hadn't looked at it like that," she said. She twisted her face into a pout.

"Most people don't." He stood on the ladder. "I'm a vet."

"Oh," she said.

Easy climbed down. "Served in Nam." He wiped his forehead with the back of his hand. "First, I was in demolition. Later a sniper. You know what that means?"

She took a step backward and shook her head.

"I could see who I killed. Not like the glory boys who dropped their bombs and turned tail. Not a tank jockey knocking down a village. Not just a grunt with a gun, sugar. I looked up their shorts. Or down their necks. On horse I could count teeth."

Her hands felt clammy. His eyes flicked over her body and back to her face.

"No need to be scared." Easy stretched his arms and yawned. "I'm done with it." He leaned back against the ladder. "Tried to kill myself once—in the VA hospital."

She put her hand on his arm. "I'm sorry."

"For what?"

"For being afraid of you."

Easy's grin split his beard and mustache. "Shit. I'm afraid of me sometimes too."

"Did you really? Kill people?"

He nodded.

"On a horse?"

He squeezed her forearm with rock-hard fingers. "Horse. Smack. Heroin! Get it?" Her flesh was white around the edge of his fingers. He let her loose. He turned his back on her and moved the ladder around to the other side of the tree. She tagged behind him. Before he could go up, she put one finger on the edge of a rose tattoo that spanned his tightened bicep.

"Was it awful?"

He let go of the ladder and stared right through her. "When you're staked out, you have to stay quiet. Horse keeps you cool—arctic cool. Nothing bothers you—not even the flies. You spot a gook. Your finger tightens. Real slow. The bullet practically oozes out of the barrel of your gun. The gook jerks. Maybe his helmet drops off. I take his gun, if he has one, or his knife—to sell to an officer for a souvenir. On horse, it's like nothing happened."

Shadow stared at his tattoo. She bit her lower lip.

"At boot camp, I became a sharpshooter—rifle and pistol. They made me an instructor. I was hot shit. I was assigned to Fort Ord. Happy as a pig in fresh manure, teaching young assholes to shoot. Breathe out easy! Fire as your breath stops. That's good! Stand ready! Fire! Again! Again! Good shooting, soldier.

"I was patriotic. Kissed the fuckin' flag. Pardon my French. Got those recruits to gun down slanty-eyed paper cutouts. A piece of cake. Living on and drinking off of Uncle Sam's easy street."

Shadow wiped sweat from her eyes.

"Then some Pentagon beanhead sent me to Nam. Worked me up in demolition. Then I was switched to one-on-one. Trained to lie in ditches, squat on rooftops, learned to shoot little yellow people who didn't know shit from Shinola. It was 'one, two three, what are we fighting for?' The TV body counts, soldier. Yes sir! F— you sir!

"I was missing my targets. Then a buddy turned me on to horse. 'Just a touch,' he said, 'you won't tremble.' Next time out, I knocked an old man off with one shot. Dropped him twenty yards from my perch. Not a waver. I sat and watched him die. Smack just kept me all easy inside."

Shadow looked into his eyes; they were unfocused, the pupils unmoving.

"After that, I was always on smack. The brass knew it. Their little killing machine was oiling himself. No problem for them! Bought my stuff off a college-boy officer. Little piss-ass Arnold never saw a day of action, never got his uniform dirty. He sold smack to pass the time. Put our money into little boxes he'd mail to himself stateside."

Easy rocked back on his heels and ran his hand through his hair. "One night I was up in a tree outside my CO's tent, higher than a hoot owl. Kept him in my sights a long time. Someone tipped him off. They sent me stateside after that—VA hospital, mental ward. Sanest thing I ever did."

He moved the ladder. "These days, I'm Mr. Mellow. I smoke dope and suck Thorazine." He positioned the ladder in a crotch between two large branches of the tree. "I live on Clayton, at Carl. Corner apartment, the one with tile above the windows. I sleep better when I can see both ways."

"I live on Clayton too," Shadow said.

"Haven't seen you around." He grinned. She saw light sparkle off a single gold tooth.

She picked up her bucket. "What do you do? I mean, you know, now."

"I'm certified one hundred percent disabled. Driven mad by the pressures of combat."

"You don't seem to be."

"I am, sugar. I'm disabled as a man can be." Easy paused. "And I'm gonna stay disabled as long as—every month—the government lays bread on me."

He started up the ladder. "Hand me my bucket, would you, sugar?"

CHAPTER 13

Lessons in merchandising

You be my Yab;
I'll be your Yum.

Scoop Nisker

A WEEK AFTER HE BOUGHT THE DIFFRACTION GRATINGS, Angelo paused outside the store. When he saw Shadow, he stepped in.

"Can you wait?" she said, glancing up and smiling at him.

She walked to the back of the store and returned with a package. "I held it for you like you asked," she said to the woman waiting at the counter.

"That's terrific!" The woman reached into a blue and black batik cloth bag. Shadow placed her small hand over the woman's fingers. "Don't worry about it. Raymundo told me your guy split. Owe it to us. Come in next week, maybe, and give us a hand."

The woman hesitated, then stuffed the package into her bag. "You guys are all right!" Her bag flung out in an arc as she whirled out of the shop.

Angelo was transfixed by the whole exchange. "You won't make much money if you don't let people pay you."

"Raymundo says we don't need to—only enough to cover our needs."

"Your salary included, I hope."

"I don't get one." She moved back behind the counter.

"I don't get it. You work for free?"

"No, I just don't get paid."

Once again, he felt as if he had fallen down a rabbit hole into Wonderland. "You don't get paid. You don't work for free. What else is there?"

"Whenever you think there are only two possibilities, you don't understand the situation. Danny Kaye said that in a movie." She wrinkled her nose. "I think it was him."

Angelo rubbed his head with both hands, smoothing down his hair nervously.

"Raymundo says, 'Take what you need from the cash drawer, but no more.' So I do get paid, kinda."

"To each according to his needs," Angelo said. He put his hands into his back pockets. "My dad would say it won't work."

"That's what his dad told him, too."

Shadow remembered Raymundo's father silhouetted against the front window, his sparse gray hair slicked down across the top of his balding head, his hands locked across his barrel chest. He glared at his son. "You're working your ass off to help a bunch—" he sputtered, trying to control himself, "a bunch of bums. You'll be out on the sidewalk before Christmas with the rest of them."

Raymundo met his father's gaze. "Dad, if you're right, then Antonio and me, we're wrong. But wow! Imagine. Try real hard to imagine that we might be right."

The older man paced, angry and silent.

"Didn't you ever give credit?" Raymundo asked.

"People I knew. People I'd grown up with. But you!" He shook his head.

"I look at their hearts."

"I'll be damned if I'll support a handout station." He stormed out, the door swinging behind him.

Raymundo walked over and closed it. Shadow joined him at the window, put her arm around his waist and gave him a hug. They watched people step aside as his father strode down the street. "I'd love to turn my Daddy on," Raymundo said.

"Maybe your dad and Raymundo's dad are right," Shadow said, shrugging. "I hope not, 'cause this is the most fun job I can think of."

"I'd miss you," Angelo said.

Silence hung between them. "I don't even know your name," Angelo said.

"It's Lol—" She took a breath. "People here call me Shadow."

"It doesn't seem to fit you. "

"Short for Shadow Dancer," she said and curtsied slightly. "What's yours?"

"Everyone calls me Angelo."

"So we have something in common," she said, shaking her head so that her hair floated over her shoulders. "Secret names."

"One of my names really is Angelo. My family doesn't like me to use it." He rubbed his head again.

"Sweeps—a guy I live with—says it's a good idea to keep your real name secret."

"Oh. . . I didn't know you were living with someone. I'm sorry. I mean, I—"

"Sweeps and me?" She giggled. "A bunch of us share a house on Clayton, that's all."

"Good." He looked intently at the floor, then back at her. "I mean. . .

never mind. I've got to go now. See you soon, Shadow."

She had moved near him. "Hope so. Hey, did you like the diffraction gratings?"

"Terrific. They were terrific."

She was almost touching him now. Suddenly she was on her toes leaning against him. He stood still, feeling the slight weight of her body on his.

Outside the store, he waved to her through the window. She waved back.

The next morning he stood in the shop doorway. "Shadow?"

"Angelo," she said, walking toward him. "What's up?"

"I've been thinking about you."

"Groovy."

"Want to take a walk later?"

She put down the records she was carrying and nodded seriously and slowly. Then her face broke into a smile. "Even groovier."

"I get off by five," he said.

"I stay till six. Then I close the store."

"I'll help."

Angelo was ironing a white shirt when Brad came in. "Hot date?" Brad asked, running his hand down the front seam.

"Taking Shadow for a walk."

"Shad who? A wispy product of your demented imagination?"

"She looks real so far."

"Turned on to you?"

"Don't know. We haven't talked much. If anything happens, rest assured I won't tell you."

"Up yours," Brad said, giving him the finger. "See if she's got a friend. I'm horny for anything with legs. Even you are starting to look good."

Shadow stood on tiptoe, her hands on Angelo's shoulders. Their faces were in shadow from the overhang on the Clayton house porch. "I loved the walk. You were so nice to me."

"Me, too."

"Will I see you again?"

He nodded.

"Soon?" He nodded again.

She took his wrists, pulled herself close. "You really listened to me," she said into his ear. "I liked that. A whole lot." She let go of his wrists.

He put his arms around her and leaned down. Their kiss was a soft brush, a delicate mix of hesitation and touching. She nestled into his shoulder, burrowed her face into his jacket. "I had a good, good time," she said.

Brad took in Angelo's good mood. "Are you, like, losing your cool?" he asked.

"She's something else. Her family doesn't even know where to find her."

"Has she got a friend? Big knockers, easy ways and oh, so lonely?"

"You make me sick."

"Just checking."

Shadow scampered up the stairs looking for Moonflower. She told her about Angelo. Moonflower chuckled. "Well, looks like you're tuned in and turned on."

"He's yummy. Super nice. He smells good. Streets full of groovy people, and I had a super time with a total square. Is that strangeness?"

"Nothing's strange if it turns you on. Nothing worth talking about if it don't. Whole houseful of menfolks was here tonight," Moonflower said, dropping deeper into her version of a Texas drawl. "And not a piece of meat worth a chew. And you—out on the streets giddy with a college boy. Lordy, lordy! Shit, honey, maybe straight is where it's at."

CHAPTER 14

The Oracle

The temple bell dies away.
The scent of flowers in the evening
is still tolling the bell.

Bashō

S HADOW OPENED THE FRONT DOOR and, seeing it was Angelo, broke into a huge smile. "I've got a terrific idea," she said.

"Should I be excited or nervous?" Angelo asked.

"Both."

"Lay it on me," he said, putting his arms around her. She wriggled loose.

"If we go to the *Oracle* office, they'll give us a bunch—for free. We sell 'em. We go pay them, and they'll give us more. Presto, we're in business."

He stiffened. "You want to sell newspapers?"

"No! I want us to sell them!"

"I can't do it."

"Did you know whenever you say 'can't,' your eyebrows go down

76

and a funny line happens right here?" She ran her finger across the center of his forehead. "How can you can't if you haven't tried?" On tiptoe, she kissed him lightly. "Please," she said, pulling at his arm like a ten-year-old. "Please, please, please."

"If we sell them, you'll just get more."

"I only have ten."

"You already went there?"

"I knew you'd say yes."

"I don't want to sell newspapers." He paled.

"Just these. I promise I won't get any more." She stroked his face. "Tonight." She pulled him down on the steps beside her and licked one of his eyes. He sighed and leaned back against the wood banister. She hopped up, leaving him slouched on the stairs. "Don't move. I'll get them."

He pictured himself waving a paper, shouting, "Read all about it! Mayor says hippies are cool. Everyone flips out! Get your paper!" His fantasy made him flush.

They walked down Clayton to Frederick and turned left going two blocks to Ashbury. Shadow bounced beside him, clutching the small bundle of papers. Most of the street was in deep shade and the sea breeze chilled him. This is dumb! So dumb!

Shadow ran out to a car stopped in traffic and tapped on the window. The driver rolled it down halfway. "Latest copy of the *Oracle*?" she said, flashing the paper.

The man rolled his window down the whole way.

Shadow shouted, "Angelo, do you have a dime?"

Wishing he were invisible, he ran out and handed her a dime. Shadow joined him back on the sidewalk a moment later. "We did it! One sold. What a team!" She bounded back out into the traffic and vanished behind a red VW bus with "Heaven's My Destination!" written in large yellow letters along one side.

A thin girl, her hair pulled back with a leather thong, came up to

Angelo. On her forehead she wore an oval diffraction grating. "The new *Oracle?*" she asked.

"Uh-huh," he said.

"Will you sell me one?"

"Hmm? Oh, sure. Fifteen cents."

She opened the small beaded leather pouch that hung from her wrist, extracted two nickels and put them in his hand. Fishing about in her pouch, she extracted three more pennies, one by one.

He hesitated before speaking. "Hey, your diffraction grating looks good."

"Is that what it's called?" She put a hand to her forehead. "Far out."

Some more shaking and poking in the girl's purse brought out one more penny. She looked up at him. "Trust me for a penny?"

"I guess so." He handed her a paper. She took it, then kissed his palm. She looked up, her lips still close to his hand. "You're my brother," she said.

Shadow reappeared, clutching her papers. "Whoopee! Two copies. This is easy. And dig it, they were friends of the God Squad, my band from Santa Cruz." She stuffed coins into his pocket. "Who was that?"

"My sister, I guess. She bought a paper. Owes us a penny."

"What would your father say?"

"I don't want to imagine."

After they sold the other papers, they walked to the *Oracle* office. Every desk was covered with piles of papers; overlapping drawings and mock-ups of pages were taped to the off-yellow walls. Shadow bought another batch of papers.

On the way down the stairs, Angelo said, "No more selling tonight. I absolutely refuse."

"You sure know how to snuff the candle of success. However—and only because I think you're terrific—I agree. Let's go home—" her eyes flashed as she lowered her voice, "and make out."

Angelo felt his face go hot and looked around to see if they had been overheard.

Shadow hefted the papers to her other arm and grabbed his hand. "No more papers tonight! Except if someone asks."

On the way to the Clayton house, she made three sales.

Later, walking home, Angelo carried a copy of the *Oracle*. Ken Kesey was on the cover, bare-chested and practically sucking a microphone. When Angelo said he didn't know who Kesey was, Shadow made him promise to read the article. As he was leaving, Sweeps told him to read Antonio and Raymundo's letter defending their way of doing business too.

"Some of the other shopkeepers don't want them here," Sweeps said. "Darkness and light are at war in the Haight. We angels may be few in number, but the game's far from over. Milton was wrong. The devil is not the most interesting character in this drama. Everything is a blessing and everything comes as a gift."

Angelo didn't know what any of that meant, but could sense that asking wouldn't raise his standing.

"Remember what Ortega y Gasset said," Sweeps continued. "'More than once you will ponder on the strange adventure which befalls truth.'"

Angelo nodded, hoping to end the discussion before Sweeps asked for his opinion.

Angelo looked into the store. He held onto the door frame with both hands, leaning in and down so that his head was level with Shadow's waist. He lifted his eyes to meet hers. "Hi, beautiful. Be my date tonight?"

"Yes! Double yes, triple yes."

"Dinner?"

"Sure. Come to the house by seven. You can help."

"No way. I want us to go out and sit down, have someone else cook it for us and bring it out. A whole different trip."

"You are unbelievably uncool."

As Angelo came over to her, she backed away. "It's so—ordinary—to go to a restaurant. Like something you do with your grandparents."

"Fair is fair. I sold newspapers with you. Tonight, you eat in a restaurant with me. Deal?"

"Can we sell papers after we eat?"

"You are such a smarty sometimes I want to punch you." He put his fist against her jaw and pushed lightly. She winced and drew back. Tears came.

"What did I do?"

She touched the place where his fist had touched her. He rubbed his hands together nervously and held them out. She ignored him.

"Tell me you're okay, or I'll feel shabby all day long."

Shadow went to him and clung to his chest. Holding onto him for balance, she rubbed her tears on his shirt. "I'm fine. Really. It's—oh." She leaned back still holding him. "Why do I keep liking you? You are so square." She stepped back.

"Don't figure it out. I'm scared that if you do, you'll toss me aside like a worn-out teddy bear."

"No chance," she said, and wiped her eyes.

When Angelo was gone, Shadow turned and ran her finger along her jaw, feeling her pulse racing. She made a fist and cautiously tapped her jaw, then hit it a little harder. The memory was no more than a bitter taste at first, then it all came back in a rush.

Her father had come home drunk enough to be surly. He'd snarled at her about her homework, which she hadn't finished. When she tried to explain, he stormed into the living room, crushing an eyebrow pencil underfoot. "Get your goddamn stuff off the floor!" he yelled. She'd hurried in. They collided in the doorway. He flailed out, hitting her flat on the jaw. She staggered back, tripped and fell.

As she lay there, weeping and holding her jaw, he bent down. "Lollie, hey kiddo, it's all right." He stroked her bare arm. She covered her face, pulled her legs up tight against her body and tried to stop crying. When he touched her again, she moaned. "Noooooo. I'm sorry. I'm sorry."

Standing up again, he stumbled slightly. "The hell with it," he muttered. He retreated back into the room, flipped on the TV and sprawled on the couch.

Shadow opened her mouth wide. "Ahhhhhh," she said as loud as she could. The sound echoed through the empty store. She moved her jaw from right to left, hard and fast, several times. She smacked her lips, swallowed and stretched out both arms. She breathed deeply and stared out the window, through the backwards letters at the top of the glass to the second-story windows across the street. A cat sat on a window ledge licking itself. She smiled.

I'll wear my Levi's tonight, she thought. They're tight in the butt, and so am I.

"How did you fit into those?" Angelo asked admiringly.

She did a pirouette. "I rubbed myself with cooking oil, then two of the guys held them for me, and I slid in."

He cupped his hands around her waist. "I don't know whether to admire you or deep-fry you." As she turned toward the door, he brushed one hand across her bottom. "How will you get out of them?"

She looked back and grinned. "I'll need help."

"Will it move if I watch?" she asked later. They lay on her mattress staring at his penis, she with undisguised fascination. Her feet, still covered by a bit of sheet, twisted back and forth. She brushed one hand across his hip.

His penis stirred, sluggishly at first, quivering as it filled, enlarging in a series of small movements, an amalgam of rising and lengthening. Firmer, it rose off his belly and straightened in small throbs.

This is definitely not Connecticut, he thought, not college, not even like the movies, not even like *one hundred dollar misunderstanding*.

"Wow," she said. "What a funny thing!"

Angelo pulled the sheet and blankets up over their naked bodies.

She nested her head on his arm. "I guess that was a lot to ask."

He nodded.

"In the shop," she said, "there's a book by a Tibetan. It says to get enlightened, meditate on the stuff that goes in and out of a body—food and drinks and snot and pee and sweat. It made me all creepy." She licked his neck just below his chin.

He turned and kissed each of her closed eyes. "Let's stop talking."

CHAPTER 15

We were never more awake

*It was as though the walls of our house
had dissolved
and my spirit had gone forth.*

R. Gordon Wasson
reporting on his first experience
with psilocybin mushrooms

MAYA KEPT MISSING HER ENTRANCES.

"Where is your mind?" the teacher asked finally.

"I'm sorry. I—"

The teacher tapped her foot. "Don't be sorry. I asked you a direct question. Center yourself. When I see you're ready, I'll let you answer."

They all laid down their instruments. Two band members left the deck and went into the kitchen. Maya sat down crosslegged on the bare wood and closed her eyes. She placed her hands on her knees, palms up, and made a circle with each first finger and thumb. She began to count her breaths from one to ten and back to one. The first few times she was distracted and missed the count. Finally she was able to go a full ten without losing awareness of either her breathing or her counting.

As Maya finished her count, the teacher said, "Now, dear one, what ruffles the surface of your mind?"

Maya opened her eyes.

"Eyes closed. Breathing calm," the teacher admonished.

Maya closed her eyes again and relaxed for another full minute before she spoke. "I'm worried about Shadow, the one who was called Lollie Anne."

"I recall her well."

"She's in trouble in San Francisco."

"You spoke with her?"

"No." Maya's breathing faltered.

"Keep your breath flowing."

"Friends saw her—selling newspapers."

"What a kind person you are, to worry so about another!"

Maya spoke again, but her voice had lost its steadiness. "I want to help her."

"And so you shall. Did your friends say she looked hungry?"

"No."

"Or even unhappy?"

Maya adjusted her posture. "No."

"But you would burst into her life uninvited and, having found fault with it, try to change it."

Maya opened her fingers.

"You may not visit her or speak with her."

Maya took a deep breath and waited.

"You may send her a postcard with your phone number."

Maya opened her eyes. "That's all?"

"Anything more is meddling." The teacher walked over and stroked Maya's forehead.

Maya tilted her face up.

"You continually forget that neither you nor she are alone. The strands that drew her to you and spun her out again are at least as real as this deck." The teacher stamped her foot. The deck shook. "I think it's time that you and the rest of the band found places to play. Audiences will curb your self-indulgence."

Maya sat bolt upright. "We're not ready."

"You are a thousand miles from being ready. But you can be stretched. Rumi says, 'Increase your necessity so that new organs of perception may appear.'" The teacher looked over at the rest of the God Squad. "You heard me. Get yourselves out there and play. If you fall on your faces, at least you'll learn to kiss the ground."

Maya turned toward the others. "Sorry, guys. Looks like my worries over Lollie Anne have put us on the road."

"I could handle getting paid for playing," Alonzo said, setting down his guitar and getting to his feet. "This music-as-spiritual-discipline stuff was getting to me anyway."

The teacher wheeled around and faced him. "For that upstart remark I've a mind to make you play the Imperlalito washboard during your first five engagements."

The boy dropped to his knees and rolled over and over. "Oh mercy, mercy, high being and beloved teacher! Cut my tongue out, stomp my picking fingers, but don't, don't make me play Mexican washboard!"

"Enough nonsense. Take a break." The teacher strode into the house. The drummer winked at the blond boy, then pulled Maya to her feet. "Years from now, this will have been the good old days," he said, looking out through the redwoods to the ocean. "You heard the lady. Time to go on the road."

CHAPTER 16

Just balling

what's too far said he
where you are said she

e. e. cummings

NITROUS EDDIE, dressed in bright yellow pants and a black vest many sizes too small, opened the door. He looked at Angelo intently, his pupils huge black shining opals.

"Is Shadow home?" Angelo asked, steadying himself against Eddie's energy.

Eddie's head rocked from side to side. "She is always home, man! At home wherever she is. The ground receives her like a seed slipping into wet loam. She is a child of this whole earth, as are any of us who remain aware of the poignant luminosity of truth." Eddie started to close the door.

"I mean, is she here now?" Angelo asked quickly.

Reluctantly, Eddie kept the door ajar. "Am I my sister's keeper who watcheth her comings and goings?" He paused for effect. "Do any of us record the passings of others? Or are we all too driven by our own solipsistic concerns to note and recollect others' doings, even those whose meals we share, whose bodies we venerate, and whose company we treasure?"

Eddie watched Angelo's body undulate. He waited until it appeared solid. "No, man," he cooed. "She is not at la casa."

"Is she coming back tonight? I know you probably don't know, but maybe you do," Angelo pleaded.

"I am getting, brother, which I think is most definitely cool, that your questions come from an open heart, a caring place, as well as personal closeness and concern for Shadow's well-being, leavened by no more than a soupçon of lust. However, I must inform you that this ain't no nuthouse, jail nor boarding school. The lady sleeps where she pleases. Tonight she pleases not to be here. Her future locations were not transmitted to me, nor to no one else."

Angelo slid his hands into his pockets. He sighed and started to walk away.

"Hey man!" Eddie rocked from side to side. "I recall that she did say if you came by, she was sorry as all get out she wasn't here but will be back tomorrow."

"Thanks for the crumbs," Angelo muttered.

"Like wow. No need to thank me. We are wasting God's own time except when we help one another. No thanks are due for natural acts. That's like thanking another soul for farting, if you get my drift."

In La Honda when the fog finally burned off close to noon, the sun shone on a man in a ragged green sleeping bag by the edge of the creek. Opening one eye, Sounder stared at the water flowing past him until he satisfied himself that it looked and behaved like water. "Guess I'm down," he said to the water. The rest of his head emerged, its fountain of dark hair falling over a high forehead and deep-set eyes. From the house he could hear Kesey's children playing noisily. He stretched, rubbed his hands over his flat belly and scratched his balls. "Food. Yes. Food's what this body wants." He scratched again. "Okay, okay! Body, stop nagging! I'll cart you up to the house and let you forage. You did me fine all weekend. It's your turn."

He pulled himself out of the bag and, standing naked in a patch of full sunlight, peed exuberantly into the creek. After shaking his penis diligently, he dug around in his sleeping bag and pulled out shorts and a pair of Levi's. Stepping cautiously on the rough stones, he ambled toward the house.

Once inside, he saw that Kesey was still asleep. Sweet Generous, almost invisible, nestled under his arm. Faye was in the kitchen doing dishes.

"Anythingtoeat?" Sounder asked her.

"What?"

"Anything—to—eat?"

"Cereal in here. Apples Sweet Generous brought are outside."

"Milk?"

"Kids got the last of it this morning."

Sounder took a bowl from the drying rack, filled it with Rice Krispies from an open box on the counter, went back outside and found the apples. He sat at the wooden table under the trees and told himself that he liked cereal without milk. The table bore the scars of the Hell's Angels' knife work from their visit a few weeks before. Sounder clicked his tongue as he read "Fouk You" and "Fucke You" among the deeply incised designs. It had been a good night, he reminded himself as he chewed and swallowed the dry Rice Krispies.

The night fog had settled in low; the forest and the mountains seemed to have been sheared off fifty feet overhead. Sounder had been up in the woods tapping out rhythms on one of Ron Boise's thunder sculptures when Shadow appeared. She began to dance to his poundings. Soon, captivated by her movements, his palm beats on the statue's metal breasts and belly matched her steps.

When he reached out to her, she'd blended into him like water flowing over grass. Too stoned to talk, he stayed quiet. When they started meandering back down the hill, he let her take the lead but bent their trail so they emerged from the forest near the shed.

Not much later, lying together on the mattress under the small window in the shed, he became absorbed in how her shoulder connected to her neck. He was sure he could see thin wires beneath her skin. He put his ear to her neck, listening to changes in her pulses as he stroked different parts of her body. After they made love, they both lay quiet, and Sounder drifted outside of time, moving without haste through fields of stars.

Shadow inched out from under Sounder's arm. Finding her shoes where he'd taken them off, she crept out and walked down to the main house. She made a space for herself among the dozen or so people watching a western on TV. Two cowboys stopped a stagecoach, but what she heard sounded like policemen tracking a drug-crazed killer through East Los Angeles. No one seemed to notice that the sound and picture didn't match.

After a while, someone got up and changed the channel to what looked like a travel film, except that something creepy was stalking the attractive young couple on the empty beach. The sounds of the earlier car chase continued, the police making smart-ass remarks between tire squeals and gunshots.

Shadow went into the kitchen. Sweeps eased himself out from the group and followed her.

"You stoned?" he asked.

"No," she said. She checked herself, "Just a little."

"Can you drive?"

"Two years, almost no accidents."

"I wanted to be back in the city tomorrow, but I'm wiped."

"Cool," she said. "I'll take us out."

Kesey was half watching the TV, his thick fingers dexterously rolling a cigarette paper. Shadow leaned over and kissed the top of his head. Almost totally absorbed in his task, he grunted an acknowledgement.

Sweeps talked about grass most of the way home. "Where there's hemp, there's hope" was his recurrent refrain. When he'd lose his train of thought, he'd mumble, "It's just a fuckin' plant, a weed that grows in the ditches along the highways in Illinois." His eyes would close and he'd snuggle into Shadow's shoulder. When he fell asleep, his head would slide off. He'd open his eyes with a jerk and begin talking again. His on-and-off ruminations kept Shadow awake as they drove up the nearly empty Highway 1 into the city.

After Sounder left the shed, he looked for Shadow. He walked around the flat end of the property near the road, then over the bridge that crossed the creek, between the parked cars, back over the bridge and finally up to the house. He touched the unpainted kitchen door with one finger and pushed off from it like a swimmer from the edge of a pool. He went back to his car. Forgetting about Shadow, he searched for his sleeping bag. Balancing the bag on his head, he walked down to the stream. He put the bag down on the bank and crawled in. Spirits of dead Indians floating under the rocks beckoned him, their long fingers reaching out of the water. He fell asleep with the sound of the stream pouring through his body.

Two nights later, in bed with Angelo, Shadow told him about the weekend. When she spoke about Sounder, he propped himself abruptly up on his elbow.

"You did what?" he asked, his voice cracking into a raspy whisper.

"I danced with this fantastic nude statue! Then the drummer and I went into this little shed and balled each other, and then—"

"I thought you loved me!"

"I do, I do. Lots!" She made a grab for him, but he scuttled to the edge of the double mattress. She crawled toward him.

"You made it with this . . . stranger?"

"Kinda." She nosed his nipple.

Angelo grabbed for his shirt.

"Hey, what's that about?" She held on to an empty sleeve, letting herself be dragged across the bed. She lunged for Angelo's hips and pulled him back down on top of her. "You can't leave! I want to make it with you! I love you so much."

"But you just did it with that other guy! Doesn't that matter?"

"Angelo, you are too weird. I'm with you. I want you! That's the way it is."

"But—" He lay back, trying to find words to match his feelings.

"It can't be any better than this." She wrapped her legs around one of his arms.

He tried to sit up. She kept him down.

"That guy in La Honda? We didn't make love. We were stoned, we grooved. That's all."

"Wasn't that enough?"

"It's over, whatever it was. Past. Gone. Poof." She blew loudly through her closed lips like a little child.

"And I'm the one who's weird?" Angelo reached for her.

"Hey, I didn't even know his name."

"Oh, that makes me feel worlds better." He rubbed his nose with a knuckle.

"You don't get it. Sometimes, you just don't get anything! But—" Her eyelids fluttered. "I'll tell you a secret." She grabbed his neck and lapped his ear noisily like a kitten slurping milk.

He squirmed. "What's the secret?"

"You're the best. The best!" Before he could answer she covered his mouth with her own.

CHAPTER 17

Easy come, easy go

There is a certain point of the mind
from which life and death,
the real and the imaginary,
the past and the future. . .
cease being perceived as contradictions.

André Breton

AT THREE IN THE MORNING, a week after Nevin had encountered Angelo, Teddy stood beside his partner outside the bathroom window at the back of the staff house. Working silently and quickly, they crisscrossed a middle pane with masking tape. Then, muffling the sound with a blanket, they used a hammer to crack the glass. Teddy reached in and rotated the sash lock. The window emitted one high-pitched creak as it slid up. They froze and waited. Then Teddy boosted Niven into the bathroom. Teddy watched him switch on a tiny flashlight, open the bathroom door and vanish into the house. Three minutes later, his long arms emerged from the window holding a typewriter. Teddy laid it carefully on the ground. Soon a second typewriter joined it.

"Pry bar," Niven whispered.

Teddy handed it up.

Moments later Teddy heard a loud crack. He scanned the windows above and listened for noises. Damn fool! Working too fast.

The pinpoint of light reappeared in the bathroom. "Bingo! Cash box. Locked. Easy with it." Teddy laid it behind the typewriters. "Hand me a sack."

Teddy passed him a cloth gunnysack. Niven was gone too long. Teddy started to sweat. The sack, when he grabbed for it, was crammed so full he could barely pull it through the window.

"What the hell?" Teddy whispered.

"They eat well here. The other sack, please. Want an almost new toaster?"

"Sure."

"Coming up."

Teddy longed for a cigarette. He pulled his collar up and rubbed his hands together, suddenly cold.

"Here."

Teddy clutched the toaster's cold smooth metal surfaces. The other sack followed.

"Give me a hand," Niven said, backing out through the window.

Together they shut the window silently and removed the blanket.

It took three trips to carry everything to the side gate. Wedging the gate open, they moved it all along the edge of the house. Teddy ran a block to the car and drove it back, letting it coast the last fifty feet with its lights and engine off. Niven emerged carrying the cash box and the toaster. Teddy pulled a back door open and went to get the sacks. On their final round, trembling as much from tension as from the effort, each carried a typewriter.

"Why'd you take so much food?" Teddy asked as they drove away.

"They had too much. Any we don't want I'll drop in a Diggers free box."

"Nothing but tenderness and concern for those less fortunate. You are a Christian gentleman. No wonder I love you."

"What the hell." Niven leaned over and gave Teddy a little kiss on the ear.

"Want a smoke?"

"Sure. Light it for me, will you," Niven said.

At the kitchen table, Teddy worked on the cash box. In a few moments he managed to break the small lock and raise the lid. Inside was a small notebook and some miniature wooden racks holding dozens of tiny glass vials.

"Not a fucking cent!" He lifted out one of the racks and read the typed label.

Sandoz Pharmaceuticals—

Investigational License #HLT 926

He coaxed out a vial and set it on the table between them. An S in a six-sided frame was etched onto the glass, and the number 1000. The liquid inside looked like water. The notebook held columns of dates and numbers, each notation followed by two sets of initials.

"Whoever said things were better than money never stole for a living," Niven said. "What do you suppose this stuff is?"

"Beats me. At least we can use the toaster." Teddy closed the box and turned it over. Stenciled in green letters he read:

PROPERTY OF U.S. GOVERNMENT

Cursing under his breath, Teddy tipped over one of the typewriters and saw an identical stencil. He smashed his fist onto the table. "The luck of the Irish," he said. "Look who we ripped off."

"Oh my God, the feds."

"Tomorrow," Teddy said. "We drive straight north, at least as far as Fort Ross. We stay there a while. I do not sleep good in a room full of U.S. government property." Niven nodded in gloomy agreement.

The next day, from a cliff on Route 1, Teddy tossed the small box toward the ocean. It clanked from ledge to ledge and came to rest in a rock cleft well above the high-tide mark. The typewriters fell all the way to the sea.

"What's the problem? Lou! You are asking me what's our problem." Bear's face gleamed with anger and frustration. "Sixty-seven thousand micrograms of d-lysergic acid diethylamide tartrate, purchased by the Central Intelligence Agency of the United States under a top-secret agreement with Sandoz Pharmaceuticals of Zurich, Switzerland, is missing plus two typewriters, an adding machine and groceries. Langwater's due back within a week. Get out before I smash your face just to cheer myself up."

Angelo called the police and asked for Officer Martin. He was told there was no Martin in the department. When he repeated the message to Bear, he was silent. Then, in a tone with more ice than fire in it, Bear said, "Stay out of my sight. Right now I'd like to murder you."

Angelo fled.

"What am I supposed to do, for Christ's sake? Langwater wants action. I've got no stuff," Bear said, more to himself than to the few staff members who'd assembled in his office.

"Can't the Evergreen Foundation send us more?" Brad asked.

"Stay out of this. You don't know a goddamn thing."

Brad and Angelo lay on their beds, each one wrapped in his own thoughts. After a while, Angelo said, "Find out how much he needs."

"Me? Give me something easy to do—like juggling flaming torches."

"I can't go near him. He blames me for everything. Just do it."

Brad asked Lou instead. "He told me that if they had as little as two thousand micrograms they could work enough johns to satisfy Langwater," Brad reported.

That night Angelo asked Shadow if she could get him that much LSD. She asked Sweeps. Sweeps asked a Digger. The Digger asked the road man for Big Brother and the Holding Company. The road man talked to Alexander Hawksmith, whose basement laboratory was the Haight's primary source of pure LSD.

It was not much acid, Hawksmith said, but the request was a strange one. A foundation using LSD? In a whorehouse? He asked the road man to check it out. Back went the question to the Digger, to Sweeps, to Shadow and to Angelo, then up the line again to Hawksmith.

Hawksmith carefully measured out twenty doses, dripping them from a pipette onto two-inch squares drawn on a piece of blotter paper. But, instead of the 100 micrograms per dose requested, he dripped out closer to 500. "Secret charity," he said to himself as he cleaned out the pipette.

Then he printed a card:

Each square = 100 mcg LSD
Soak in distilled H_2O three minutes to release.

Satisfied with the display of scientific formality and amused by his donation of a massive overdose, he put the blotter paper and the card into a large manila envelope. On the outside he printed, in the same draftsmanlike hand:

FOR INVESTIGATIONAL USE ONLY.

He gave it to the road man, who passed it to the Digger, who took a square for himself before he handed it on to Sweeps. Sweeps gave it to Shadow, who presented it to Angelo.

Holding the envelope, Angelo walked down Clayton and back to the staff house. He entered Bear's office.

"What the fuck do you want?" Bear said.

"You need some stuff for Dr. Langwater's visit. Here."

Bear took the envelope and looked inside. "What is it?"

"LSD."

"What the hell am I supposed to do with it? Eat the paper?"

Angelo showed Bear the card.

"How'd you get hold of this?"

"I've made a few friends."

"How do I know it's real?"

"See where one square's torn away? Someone tried it along the way."

"I suppose you want a medal."

Angelo stood, suppressing a smile.

"First you get us robbed. Now you cover your ass. Okay, you're square. Now fuck off."

Angelo went up the stairs two at a time. "He couldn't stand being grateful," he told Brad as he flopped down on his bed. "He was almost nice to me. Almost." He sat up and laughed. "But he controlled himself."

CHAPTER 18

White Lightning

As far as we can discern,
the sole purpose of human existence is
to kindle a light in the darkness
of mere being.

Carl Jung

ANGELO CAME BY THE HOUSE one night and found that Shadow was out. Nitrous Eddie appeared pleased with his disappointment. "She and Moonflower flittered to the East Bay. The big-breasted thrush is trying out for a band. 'Waste of time,' says I. She says to Shadow, 'Come be my lucky piece.' 'You're a lucky piece yourself,' says I. 'Fuck you,' she says. The woman is all class!"

Instead of going back to his house, Angelo wandered down to the Panhandle. Ringed by a small circle of people, a band was rehearsing under a big leaf maple still holding on to its last red and yellow leaves. "Skill and Bones" was written in black and red letters across the face of their bass drum. Angelo sat and listened as the band ran through several tunes. The headman on guitar, in the middle of the third song, yelled at a band member. "Pick it up, motherfucker! For Christ sake, pick it up."

A short girl wearing a beaded headband leaned over. "Had enough?" she asked Angelo.

"You bet."

"Let's pick it up and get out of here."

"Fine by me."

Walking down the Panhandle toward the park, she told him her name was White Lightning, and her father was a lawyer and on the Oakland City Council. "He disapproves of everything I think or say or do."

"Sounds like my parents—or would, if they knew, I guess. I'm from Connecticut. My dad works on Wall Street, near it actually."

White Lightning rubbed her bare arms. "It's getting cold. I've got a mess of spaghetti at my place asking to be cooked. Want some?" Her hip slid against his.

"Best offer I've had this week."

She took out a yellow tablet from her bag, broke it into two and put one in her mouth. "Want a half?"

"What is it?"

"Whew, you are from Connecticut! Genuine Hawksmith acid. No cheap street shit for White Lightning." She held out the broken tab. "I scored a batch a while back—high friends in high places."

"No thanks, I had some last week—on blotter paper," he said, acutely aware of his inability to sound casual.

"That's cool," she said, and ate the other half.

The spaghetti sauce was a family recipe, she told him as they ate. Her family had been in California for over a hundred years. More of them trickled in from Milano every generation. "Daddy's a straight-ass lawyer and dresses and talks like we've got class, but we come from fifty generations of dirt people."

When she asked what he was doing in San Francisco, he managed to change the subject and talked about the people at the house on Clayton. "When they're stoned, I can't understand half of what they're saying."

"Who says making sense is where it's at, baby? When I'm stoned, I don't give a flying flip if I make sense. Think like a scat singer. I do—do da, di, di di, di dum-dum." She imitated a trumpet and, still singing, pulled him up from the table and danced against him. "Like now," she whispered.

She danced round and round him, kissing him deftly on each turn. Later, as they lay together in the semidarkness, she lit a candle.

"What's that for?" he asked.

"The flicker gives me the rhythm."

When they began to make love, she anticipated his every movement. She blended to him, moved without hesitation. She fit herself under him, beside him, around him. She made him feel as if his own movements had acquired perfect grace.

They had become a single being—a bivalve of pleasure. She sustained him at the edge of orgasm over and over. Each time he'd feel he was gone, she'd release their energy. The moment he regained control, she led him into another round of excitement. Finally, they came together inside the same breath.

After he napped for a few minutes, they started again. She moved him into long waves of sustained excitement. He lost awareness of himself, conscious only of pulsations of pleasure.

In the morning, they made love again, but the harmony was gone. She was slow at first, even hesitant. She held him, pulling his hips into hers. She came first, then pumped him to a climax. He slid off her, disconcerted.

"Last night—" he said, as they got dressed.

She laughed and slapped him on the shoulder. "When White Lightning is riding acid, she's the queen of the night. Ain't it the truth!" Her laughter grated on him. Last night her feet had seemed so soft and sensitive. But this morning, he saw her heels were laced with cracks and there were patches of dried skin peeling away.

She flexed her toes. "Told you I was a peasant." She laughed loudly. "Angelo, what do you do?"

"I'm part of a research team."

"Far out!"

"It's pretty dull, actually," he said, looking under her bed for his other sock.

"Not studying hippies, I hope."

"No," he said, finding it. "Nothing like that."

"A fast crap, and I'm off to my stupid little job." She leaned over and touched his face. "Am I gonna see you again?"

"You bet," he said. He pulled her close and kissed her deeply. She sighed, pulled away slowly and vanished into the bathroom. He called after her.

"Lightning. I'm out. See you."

"Bye-bye, sweet American pie."

He hurried back through the park and up the Panhandle. Shadow was right. He was a square. A four-sided square. That last kiss—laah! Like a machine. Damn it all, he literally had lied through his teeth. Sauce for the gander, Shadow. She had her fuck in the woods. He made it with White Lightning. She called it freedom! Not for him.

That night he told Shadow everything, except how wonderful it had been at first. When he stopped talking, she leapt into his arms. "You are so delicious. How come you've picked me?"

"Because I'm too square to be with anyone else?"

She kissed his face. "Were her breasts bigger than mine? Bet they were! Mine are just little poops."

"Big squashy wads."

"Now you make her sound gross."

"I want you. Want to be with you."

"You don't mind little breasts?"

"Try me."

CHAPTER 19

Sweeps listens

*I don't understand
why half the world is still cryin'...
when the other half of the world
is crying, too.*

Janis Joplin

CAN'T YOU STAY?" Shadow asked, alternately stroking and kissing Angelo's shoulder.

"I told you—the big boss is here. All hands on board."

"Well, then. So much for you. I'm splitting before you can leave me." Sliding over the bottom sheet, she wriggled half of her naked body onto the floor. The roughness of the rug's nap scrubbed at her forearms and chest. She purred as she burrowed into it. Angelo grabbed after her, catching an ankle. Her fingers dug into the rug. He easily pulled her back onto the mattress.

"Beast!" She giggled. "Let me go!" Her voice was shrill.

Still laughing, he took her other ankle and flipped her over, staring at her smooth calves, her narrow thighs and her dark puff of pubic hair. Gazing up at her, he was stunned to see tears making damp streaks down her face.

He slid quickly up the bed. "Did I hurt you?"

She crawled back against the wall and curled into a ball. "No." She pulled the top sheet up to her face and reached for the blanket, pulling them both over her head.

Angelo was on his knees. "Shadow?" He put a hand on the blanket over her hips.

"I'll be okay." Even muffled by the covers, he heard the trembling in her voice.

He stroked the raised blanket. "I'm sorry for whatever I did."

Coming out from the covers, she clamped one arm around his neck and shoulder. She wiped her eyes with her other hand and pulled her hair off her face. She stared up into space. Her hair, fanned out on the pillow, framed her tear-streaked face. Finally she looked up at Angelo.

"Don't die," she whispered. "Don't die."

"Hey." He waved his hands in front of her face. "It's me—Angelo. I'm very much alive."

She reached up to stroke his face. "Just a bad memory."

"Want to tell me?"

"Not really."

Her breathing became more regular, and soon her eyes closed. He rolled onto his side and held her closely. When he gently removed his arm from under her head a few minutes later, her breathing didn't change. He dressed quietly and left.

Later she awoke. Unable to get back to sleep, she wandered about the house, hoping someone would notice her. She poured herself a glass of milk and went up to talk to Sweeps.

He listened patiently. "What happened?"

With a sigh, she sat down next to him. "When he grabbed my ankle, all I could feel was Dad doing that to me."

Sweeps nodded the way he'd learned to do when anyone explained something to him. Several Stanford professors had concluded that he'd been fascinated by their lectures, when in fact he'd neither understood nor cared about what they were saying. Then, like now, he was truly trying to be kind.

"I guess I was eight," Shadow said. "Daddy was yelling at Mom. She kept pleading with him to go to bed. I couldn't hear what he said. I held my blanket tight and started crying, not real loud, but enough. Mom told him he'd woke me. He told her to shut up, that she was the one who made him shout.

"I heard a noise and then a sob. He must have hit her. I heard Mom run into the bathroom, a klunk when she shut the door and a clickety-click when she locked it.

"I stayed way under the covers. I heard a chair fall over and Dad stumble around. He knocked on the bathroom door—not a real knock. It was a scrape, like a dog makes when it wants to be let out.

"He told her she should come out, not to be scared. Then he sort of slapped at the door. 'Come out of there. Now!' He was shouting again. He banged on the door and said, 'Come out or I'll bust the handle off.'

"I could hear every word. He started beating on the door. Bang, bang, bang, bang. Louder and louder. Bang, bang, bang!"

Sweeps nodded and put out his hand. Shadow took it and held it to her cheek.

"Then he stomped out to the living room." She put an imaginary phone to her ear and her finger made circles in the air. "Click, click, click. Click, click, click, click. I heard him say, 'Hello? Is this the police department? I think my wife has hurt herself, maybe even killed herself.' Then he clunked the phone down.

"I started crying so hard I could hardly see. I ran out of my room to the bathroom door. 'Mommy, Mommy,' I screamed. 'Don't die!'"

Sweeps put his arm around Shadow and cradled her head on his shoulder. She sat crying softly and sniffling as she spoke. "I stood there in my nightie, beating on the door and screaming. The next thing I remember is that I was in the air, upside down! Dad was holding me—by my ankles."

She shuddered. "I remember I said, 'Don't kill me!' He swung me back and forth, holding me out. He was laughing so hard he spattered me with spit. I thought he was going to slam me against the wall, but he carried me back to my room and threw me on my bed, laughing like it was the biggest joke in the world.

"He never had called the police—that was just pretended. I still have nightmares where Mom's being hurt and I can't get to her."

She let Sweeps hold her for a long time.

PART III

CHAPTER 20

Flo's sitting this one out

Distortion of reality
is an effect attributed to the
psychedelic drug LSD.

Dr. Hip (Eugene Schoenfeld, M.D.)

ALL FIVE OBSERVATION CUBICLES had been cleared, cleaned and readied. As Bear predicted, Langwater demanded a session the night he arrived.

Twittering and chirping, Langwater was everywhere, demanding to be told every detail. During dinner in the staff house, he poured himself glass after glass of cognac from a bottle he took from a flight bag he'd placed under his chair. By the end of the meal his hands had stopped fluttering and his small bony shoulders didn't arch toward his neck every time he spoke. "You know, you're not the only location we have working on this," he said.

"Other setups like us?" Bear asked.

"Extracting information has gone far, very far." He patted the paper napkin across his thin lips, folded it into exact thirds and laid it on the table.

Each square of blotter paper had been soaked in water. Brad had squeezed the liquid one by one into a beaker and stored it in the refrigerator the night before. In the morning, he had poured the contents evenly into nineteen compartments of a twenty cube ice tray.

"One cube with a shot of whiskey for the first ten customers. The next ten get whiskey with ordinary ice; the next nine, special ice again," Bear told the girls.

Flo, who at twenty-nine was the oldest girl working, looked at him from under her heavily made-up deep-purple eyelids. "That's a lot of funny ice. What's the deal?"

"You got guests, we got guests. We want two shifts. Get it?"

"Got it."

Several times while they waited, Langwater sprang up, went downstairs and peeked through the viewing slot into the living room. "A few Negroes in there with the others, and a Jap. One man's hair is long as a girl's," he reported.

The observers took off their jackets, loosened their ties and settled down. Langwater flitted from room to room, perching on the edges of chairs, scattering papers. He made no effort to suppress his excitement, pushing his nose against the glass to look into a room. Then he'd race to another room, his black coat flapping behind him.

Each customer was given bourbon on ice. The girls chatted with the men until the ice had melted and the men had finished their drinks. Gradually they paired off and went upstairs. The observers sat in their cubicles, clipboards in hand, checking their watches every few minutes and recording what they saw.

Forty minutes after he'd walked into Room Two, a sailor with a beer belly and no hair on his arms or chest suddenly shouted, "I can't find my dick. Someone stole my dick!" The girl at his side tried to quiet him, but he pushed her away. Holding onto his penis, he got out of bed and hollered, "It's gone! This ain't my dick!" He bounded into the hall and beat on the next door. "One of you got my dick!"

In Room Three, a man who said his name was Fred was about to start intercourse when he heard the shout. He looked down at himself and hooted with laughter. "Tommy," he called out. "I'm checking! I'm checking. The one I'm using sure looks like mine." He laughed again and looked into the face of the girl on the bed. Then he squinted and rubbed his eyes. "You shit as hell look like my sister." He flung himself off her. "Not my fault she died. Everybody knows that!" He backed off the bed, his hands pushing at empty space, his eyes wide.

Tommy was still in the hall hollering.

"I'm not your sister. That's crazy talk. Come on, now." The girl held out her arms. Fred moved backward until he was against the wall. "Your hands—claws, not hands. Your face— Stay where you are. Oh God." He shuddered. "You're so beautiful." He moved toward her open arms, rubbing at his eyes with his fingers. He stopped, and rocked back on his heels. "I'm going fucking crazy," he whispered.

A man's voice could be heard from Flo's room. "Allen Funt is a Jewish cunt," he shouted over and over. Flo appeared in her doorway wearing a short red silk robe. She walked to the nearest bathroom. "The hell with it," she said. "Flo's sitting this one out." She went in and locked the door.

In Flo's room, the man started taking the pictures off the walls. "Unnecessary. Unnecessary." He piled them in the center of the floor. After he'd stripped the walls, he noticed the glass animals on her dresser. He looked each one over, pronounced it unnecessary and carefully placed it on top of the pile of pictures.

Flo finished her cigarette. Hearing nothing, she unlocked the bathroom door and walked to her room. "What the fuck are you doing, buster?" she screamed. The man was holding her pillowcase. "Unnecessary," he said to her, and draped it over the animals.

"You're unnecessary!" she hissed, and shoved him into the hall. A moment later she opened the door long enough to kick his clothes out. The man, wearing boxer shorts, stood transfixed, staring at the pile of clothes at his feet. Finally he leaned over, picked them up, walked to the edge of the staircase and tossed them over. "Unnecessary." Turning back, he collided with Tommy.

"Did you take my dick?" Tommy asked.

"Unnecessary," the man said, reaching inside his own shorts, however, to verify the truth of his statement.

The Japanese American in Room Six, who had boasted to the girl that he had a master's degree in Romance languages from Berkeley, was sitting in the center of the bed, breathing slowly and deeply. Then he began reciting the opening stanzas from Dante's Inferno.

Langwater, in the observation room, muttered, "Japs are tough."

Fred had come back to bed. His partner, much to his surprise, had climaxed with him. They lay together, her hands stroking his heavily muscled neck and shoulders. Fred stared into space, apparently oblivious to both her and the increasing volume of screams, thumps and shouts outside the room.

Several men in the hall were holding each other and praying. The girls who'd been able to get downstairs were packed into one end of the living room, consoling one another. Flo stayed in her room, telling the universe what she thought of men in general and Bear in particular.

Langwater put his nose flat up against the glass and watched Fred.

Inside the room, Fred stared at the large dark smudge that had appeared on the surface of the mirror. "What's that?" he said, pointing.

"What's what?" the girl answered.

"That." The smudge vanished. Fred jumped out of bed, stood in front of the mirror and shook his head like a dog. His cheeks flapped against his teeth and he snarled, "Buuuuuuuewwww."

"Come back here," the girl said, raising herself on one elbow.

Langwater stood back from the glass.

Pressing one eye against the mirror, Fred stared through the clouded glass. A line of light flickered, then disappeared. Fred pressed on the glass with both hands. He scanned the edges of the mirror and shoved again. He banged on it and made it rattle. Then he wrapped his T-shirt tightly around his fist and smashed it into the mirror. The pane shattered. Langwater and Fred were suddenly eye to eye.

Fred punched again. Glass shards spewed into the observation room. Bleeding from a long gash on his forearm, Fred staggered back. The girl screamed. Fred tore a leg off a chair and knocked the remaining shards from the frame. The girl fled.

Tommy was still asking after his dick. "I don't know, buddy," Fred shouted. "But I'll show you where they took it." Tommy ran in. Fred stood naked, a chair leg in one hand, a bloody shirt in the other. Blood dripped down his arm and spattered over his legs and feet.

"Nooooooo!" Tommy wailed, and ran back into the hall.

In three steps Fred was at the hole in the wall. He stepped over the frame, avoiding the few shards still embedded in it. He tried the door, now locked from the outside. He slammed his shoulder against it, then picked up the chair leg and smashed it into the door. After two blows, the thin wood gave. He punched out enough of the door to shove his hand through, fumbled for the handle and unlocked it.

In the narrow hall, Langwater spread his black overcoat and blocked the hallway light. "I am your death," he screeched, raising his arms higher. As Fred spun to face him, Bear struck him from behind at the base of the neck. Fred fell heavily to one knee. Bear hit him again, and he fell face down onto the carpet.

"Quick! Tie him up!" Langwater shrieked, retreating down the hall.

"He'll stay out for a while," Bear said, rubbing his knuckles. "Jesus. He's bleeding like a pig. Langwater, you're a doctor. Do something!"

Langwater inched forward and unwound the shirt from Fred's hand. "Messy, messy. This will need stitches."

"I'll get help."

"No. I'll go." Langwater scuttled away.

"Fucking coward," Bear muttered. He pressed two fingers on Fred's arm above the wound.

Langwater dialed Letterman Military Hospital, uttered a single code word and let loose a string of orders.

Ten minutes later, a military ambulance pulled up beside the house. Two medics emerged, followed by two soldiers carrying rifles. The front door flew open, and a stream of half-naked men poured out and scattered like ants from a broken anthill. In the midst of the pandemonium, Brad called to the medics. "In here."

A few minutes later they reappeared carrying Fred tightly tied to a stretcher with wide khaki-colored straps.

"Easy does it," Langwater said as they worked the stretcher down the stairs to the street. "These boys are taking you to a hospital," he said to Fred. "You fell. Just fell. Hit your head and cut your arm. Hard to remember—very hard to remember. Hit your head. Hit your head."

Fred's eyes were glazed. "Thanks," he said. They lifted him into the ambulance.

Langwater turned to the soldiers. "Get him stitched, get him dressed, get him out of the hospital. Set him down in the Marina near Fort Mason. Am I clear?"

The soldier relaxed his grip on the stock of his rifle. "Yes, sir. Got it, sir."

"Here are his clothes and his wallet. I know how much money is in it. Be sure it's all there when he is released."

"Yes, sir."

"Full report to this number by eight hundred hours." He held out a piece of paper. The soldier took it and stuck it into his shirt pocket.

"One last thing, soldier. I want no written record of this pickup. You found this man on the street, dazed and bleeding."

"Yes, sir. I'm in Intelligence, sir."

"Good. Use some."

CHAPTER 21

Dr. Langwater's version

Does it matter how long
a rock soaks in water;
will it ever grow soft?

Basavanna

UNABLE TO STILL THE CHORUS of tears and insults, Bear told the girls to knock it off, lock the front door and go to bed. Then he joined his staff in the kitchen who were talking to one another in low tones. Langwater poured himself a cup of coffee, then topped it off from his cognac bottle. "Gentlemen," he said. "Let us consider what has happened." He paused to inhale the fumes from his cup. Everyone was seated except Bear, who stood behind Langwater in the open doorway.

"Our invisibility, which we have labored to create and maintain in this location, has been badly compromised. At least one of the evening's guests is at this moment being treated for injuries. At the same time a number of men have been let loose, still metabolizing a powerful psychotomimetic and subject to all the psychic disturbances inherent in such an ingestion, including unknown factors occasioned by leaving this monitored, secure setting.

"Next door, a cluster of badly disturbed young women, whose livelihood depends on their ability to be relaxed and convivial, are, if I may be forgiven for using an inelegant phrase, emotional trash. Some of these ladies of the evening may require therapeutic intervention before they will willingly return to their occupation.

"Three of the five observation rooms were broken into. Furniture, recording devices, in fact the very doors of these rooms, are in pieces. To repair the damage will be expensive. Your current funding ostensibly comes, as some of you know, from the largess of several foundations. Their freedom of action, their very existence, depends on a lack of public scrutiny. None of these foundations will be eager to allocate dollars for the reconstruction of a damaged house of prostitution."

When Lou looked over, Bear was staring off into space.

"I would be hopeful, gentlemen—most hopeful, if I were you—that the local press does not learn about this evening. If publicity were to arise, the funding groups and the Agency itself would disavow the project."

Brad slid a note over to Angelo. "Agency?" Angelo shrugged. He wrote a few question marks on the paper and passed it back.

"They would, in fact, deflect public outcry by accusing you of unauthorized and potentially criminal activity, including illicit sexual experimentation. There might be criminal charges. An eager local prosecutor, intent on self-promotion, might add charges of pandering, along with the desecration of the minds of young males seeking nothing more than simple sexual relief."

Langwater began to assemble a sandwich of ham slices, lettuce, mustard and mayonnaise.

"Many of your customers serve in the military, and are engaged in a rather robust and full-spirited, if unpopular, war. Your antics, gentlemen, might be viewed as an attempt to destroy the effectiveness of military personnel. Any legal proceedings or public disclosure would tantalize the antiwar fanatics and, at the same time, bring on the virulent hatred of those who love the American soldier."

Langwater bit into the sandwich and chewed with gusto, his mouth partly open.

"Now of course each of you can ask yourself," he said, waving his sandwich, "'Was I even partly responsible for what occurred?' Each of you will doubtless find yourself blameless. Then you will decide whom you can blame. If you are ordinary and conventional, and most of you are, you will attack both ends of your pecking order, first turning on Bear. You will say that it was by his orders and under his guidance that this occurred. That will avail you nothing. You will then turn on these boys—" he gestured toward Angelo and Brad, "whose work, little valued as it is, has been nothing more than serving an organization whose very title has been withheld from them. They, in their turn, will attack you all."

Langwater finished his sandwich. No one else moved. Wiping his mouth, he said, "While you may do all this, I can assure you that in my report I will neither encourage nor condone such mean-spirited avoidance of responsibility. Instead, I will indicate that this evening had all the earmarks of full-scale collaboration."

Several people started to speak. Langwater silenced them with a wave of his cup. "You are about to protest that you and you and you had nothing to do with this." He pointed with his cup at various staff members. "You may even be able to convince yourselves.

"For those of you who hope to continue with the Agency, you have my word that a full description of this performance shall be entered into your permanent records." He made himself another sandwich, then cut it into thirds.

As if oblivious of the effects of his remarks, Langwater got up and poured himself another cup of coffee. He held the pot out, offering it to the group. No one touched their cup.

Bear leaned forward. "Dr. Langwater," he said. "I don't think you got it right. Let's sort things out in the morning."

Langwater slowly rotated his cup, his thin hands turning pink from the warmth. "I'm not tired. But then again I was only an observer. I had no part in either the preparation or the execution of this evening's ill-fated prank." He pushed his chair back. With his skinny neck extended, his thin shoulders hunched high, his black coat pressed up against his cheeks, he looked more like a vulture than ever.

"You." He pointed a narrow finger at Angelo's chest. "Do you have a car?"

"Yes, sir."

"Where is it?"

"A couple of blocks away, sir. Bear doesn't like—"

"I am not interested in Ralph's likes and dislikes. Go and get it. You will take me to a hotel." Angelo pushed his way out of the kitchen.

Langwater widened his gaze to include the whole group. "I know I have a room set aside for me, but isn't it evident that we shall all sleep more easily tonight if I am somewhere else?"

He stood up, his sandwich untouched, walked out of the kitchen and up the stairs. Angelo was at the front door when he descended the staircase, a suitcase in each hand. Angelo held the door open, then followed him out.

In the kitchen, someone said, "What a rotten bastard!"

"Shitty little crow," another said.

Bear dragged over a chair. "Tomorrow morning, before the girls are up, get the broken glass cleared away. Cover the holes in the rooms with blankets."

"What did we give them?" someone asked.

"LSD, as usual," Lou answered curtly.

"Maybe it was Langwater's fault," someone else said. "He's some kind of witch doctor."

"Yeah. If it was anyone's fault, it was his."

The group laughter was forced and bitter.

"The car's not real clean, sir," Angelo said as he opened the rear door.

"Nothing I've seen this evening is. Do you know the Mark Hopkins?"

"No. I'm from Connecticut."

"I will direct you."

In the darkness Angelo couldn't be sure, but it looked to him as if Langwater was smiling.

CHAPTER 22

Wait until the rocks stop moving

From time to time
The clouds give rest
To the moon-beholders.

Bashō

EARLY THE FOLLOWING MORNING the ground fog had lifted almost everywhere else, but it still clung to the bottoms of the small valleys in Golden Gate Park. There was not enough light yet to give color. Everything was in silhouette, and the trees, still black, seemed pasted onto a glistening gray sky.

Nitrous Eddie, walking back from a party, was deliberately weaving from one side of the path to the other. He'd overdosed on donuts and potato chips to appease the ravenous hunger that came over him after he'd been smoking dope all night. "But," he heard himself say, as if another voice inside had been given permission to speak, "if you hadn't smoked so much dope, you wouldn't have had the munchies." He listened to a second voice. "Stop whining! Munchies go with the territory.

Your gut will recover in hours. But the dope residuals will circulate in your blood for days—days!" Buoyed up by this, Eddie accepted the immediate physical discomfort.

Approaching a rise, he saw two men in what appeared to be military uniforms off to the side of the path. They tried to hide behind two trees, neither of which was thick enough around to conceal even a child.

"Peekaboo, I see you," Eddie said.

"Help," one of the men said.

"Shut up, Tommy," the other said.

Eddie stopped and watched them. They stayed behind the trees. "How about—I help you, then shut up?" Eddie opened and displayed his empty palms in what he recalled was a universal gesture of peace and goodwill.

The two men slowly emerged from the trees and walked toward him. Tommy wore one shoe; the other man had a jacket but no shirt.

"You guys been out here long?" Eddie asked, trying to sound casual.

"Everything is moving," Tommy said.

"Since earlier tonight," the other man said.

Eddie thought this through five or six times. "You stoned?"

They looked at each other. "What's that?" Tommy asked.

Eddie scratched his nose. He had never been asked to explain, especially while stoned himself. "Everything going funny?"

"Yeah. We were in this house." The other man punched Tommy in the gut. "Had a few drinks." He backed up. "Shit! I can see through your head."

Eddie raised both hands and touched the sides of his head, a gesture he'd learned from a full-blooded Cheyenne. It meant, "We all understand one another." He said, "I know what you mean, man. It's like falling down the rabbit hole." He opened his arms. "Eddie's going to help you."

The two men looked around.

"That's me." Eddie pointed to a small hill beside them topped with a circle of large stones and a small grove of Monterey pines. "We go up here." Eddie walked them up the hill.

"Each of you sit on a stone," he said. They did.

"Now you are properly stoned." Eddie peered into their eyes. He sighed. They understood humor, he realized, as little as they'd understood sign language. "How'd you get this way?"

He listened to the fragments of their story with growing compassion. What little sense it made sounded to Eddie like a terrible betrayal. He believed strongly that there was an inherent blessing in using a psychedelic. He hated to see that opportunity misused or squandered. "In my opinion, which is highly personal and may not be appreciated by those of greater wisdom, I would say—and mind you, this is only speculation—you guys have been royally fucked over."

They both nodded.

"We've been hiding," Tommy said.

"I told you Eddie would help and help he shall. Each of you, look close at your stone! It's probably moving."

They lowered their heads and looked between their legs at their stones. Each nodded.

"Yeah, that's cool," Eddie said. "Moving, but not much. Rocks move real slow." They looked up at him, innocent as children. "In a while, the stones will stop moving. You dig?"

"They're moving," Tommy said.

"Kinda quivering," the other man said.

"That's cause they're alive," Eddie said.

Tommy jumped up.

"Hey! It's all cool." Eddie waved him back to his stone. "They like being sat on. It makes their day. They'll talk about it in rock talk for forty, maybe fifty years. It's a fantastic groove to have you guys on them."

Tommy sat back down uneasily.

"So, you stay here. Soon the sun is going to make a major breakthrough. Little birds will come around. They're cool. All the stuff around here is cool. That's why Eddie put you guys here. This is a supersafe place.

"Depending on how much righteous shit you took, after a while the rocks will stop moving. That's how you'll know you're down."

"After the rocks stop?" Tommy asked.

"Then we're normal," his friend said.

"I'd never slander a fellow creature by calling him normal, but you'll be down, way down. Then you can leave your rock buddies. Before you blow down the hill, however, you thank them. They'll dig it. Then go get a bus or whatever you guys do."

They looked at one another and then back at Eddie.

"You watch each other's rocks. That's how you'll know. The trees'll move, the grass may crash around a bit. It all moves, but it's all cool. When the rocks stop moving, everything's smooth as butter."

Eddie bowed and headed down the hill. At the bottom he waved to the men. He kept waving, hand over his head, back and forth, until he was out of sight.

CHAPTER 23

A Human Be-In

I build the bridge of heaven and the bridge of earth.
I erect a bridge between this world and the next.
I raise the bridge of the seven stars. . .

Invocation of a Yao shaman

January 14, 1967

CHANTS ROLLED UP THE HILLS of the Haight and broke against the buildings. Everyone was in motion. The earth undulated under bare and sandaled feet moving toward the park. The morning fog had withdrawn to the ocean, leaving a bright day, clear edged and glittering as cut crystal.

Angelo and Shadow walked holding hands, she out of simple affection, he to ensure that she wouldn't wander off. From time to time, he pulled her close as if his arm was a leash. The noisy good cheer and easy affection of the crowd made him edgy. Moonflower, sensing his uneasiness, left the two of them behind almost as soon as they started walking.

Two men, both shirtless, stopped to admire Shadow. One wore an open vest, red and white stripes in front, white stars on a blue field on the back. The other sported a black top hat with a sky blue band. Shadow tilted her head and did a pirouette.

Vest flashed her a victory salute.

"Go for it!" Top Hat said.

"I am it!" she said.

Vest shook his head like a dog shaking off water. "Whoooooeeeee."

Angelo tugged Shadow along.

If one could see it from the air, this part of the park looked like a colony of brightly colored ants feeding on a tray of green icing. People everywhere, frolicsome as puppies, rubbed, stroked and fondled each other, greeting one another with expansive hugs and deep kisses.

Angelo and Shadow walked up to the high side of the meadow close to the trees, where they could see over the heads of the thousands of people streaming in from all sides. Among the trees but out of sight, mounted police sat alert in their saddles, taking care not to provoke the very disturbances they might need to quell. After Angelo pointed them out, Shadow stared into the trees. "Not going to bug us, it looks like," she said.

Angelo pulled her down to the grass beside him. "Now you be cool."

"Just blowing them good vibes," she said. Crawling onto his lap, she held his head to her breasts. "Trying to turn you on," she whispered.

"One hundred percent success!" he said.

She smiled in delight.

"When will the poetry start?" Angelo asked no one in particular.

A gray-bearded man passing below them overheard the question. He wore faded patched overalls, one of the straps replaced by a paisley tie. He marched a few steps up the hill, squatted and grinned, displaying a mouth with more holes than teeth. "Hey, buster! It started a million years ago. This is just a reunion. When anybody walks, that's dance. When anybody speaks, that's poetry! You dig?" He settled down on the grass below them with a soft bump.

Shadow nodded cheerfully. Angelo held her like a shield. The man

looked from one to the other. "You'll do. Alfred the Agile says you'll do."
Then, slowly and ceremoniously, he rolled over backwards—once, twice
and a third time, down the hill. Ending in a crouch, he rose in a single
smooth motion and walked away.

"What a beautiful old guy!" Shadow said. Her gaze followed him
down the lawn. Alfred passed by a child, cheeks painted with stars and
rainbows with circles painted around each eye. She stuck out her tongue
at him. He responded with a full extension of his own tongue. She
backed up two steps toward her parents. As he moved on, he gave her another tongue flick, like a frog snagging a fly.

"He was examining us," Angelo said. "I think I passed only because
I'm with you."

"Aren't you grateful?" Shadow slid off Angelo's lap. She wrapped her
arms around her knees and cocked her head like a bird, turning it in little jerks, focusing on one group after another. Suddenly she was gone,
darting over and around people, down the hill and up the other side.

The major construction had been completed—the stage built, toilets set
up, the bands' generators on flatbed trucks parked behind the trees.
Power cords thick as men's arms linked the trucks to the stage like great
black sea serpents at rest.

Sweeps walked down the hill. He had been working at the site since
early morning. He talked the park people into lending them thin stakes
and plant wire to secure the cords. Someone deposited a pack of prayer
flags on the stage; Sweeps climbed the trees behind the stage and tied
them to high branches.

He had taken a few tokes off a hash pipe offered by a Hell's Angel as
they laid cables together. Now the sunlight on the damp grass looked like
the surface of the sea. He felt as if he were walking on the exposed edge
of a tropical reef teeming with schools of brightly colored fish.

Earlier, like a small child following a parade, Sweeps had tagged along when Gary Snyder and Allen Ginsberg circumambulated the meadow chanting, "Om Om Om, Sa Ra Wa, Buddha Dakini Yeh Benzo Wa Ni Yeh." Sweeps was especially attracted to Ginsberg, whose glistening bald head rose out of his full black beard like a lotus from a muddy pond. Even in spotless white pants and a white Indian shirt, Ginsberg still looked like a Jewish intellectual. Gary Snyder walked beside him in pants that were too small, a pale green pullover, a string of wooden beads and one earring so long it was submerged in his beard. Other chanters walked with them, including several affluent hippies sporting elegant boots and woven wool capes. Sweeps stayed within earshot but out of range, not letting himself become part of the group. Nor could he muster enough self-determination to leave them as long as they were chanting.

Father O'Malley, sitting by himself next to a power cable, nodded to Sweeps as he passed. Sweeps returned the nod but didn't consciously connect the slight young man in the faded shirt and jeans with the Catholic priest he'd met. Nearby, Moonflower was loudly making herself a center of conversation.

As Sweeps trailed after the chanters, he watched himself with a touch of irony. Still following literary figures! Be reborn a thousand times, and he'll still be an asshole graduate student. He chanted, "Sa Ra Wa, Sa Ra Wa," and was still chanting when Shadow came up and tugged at him from behind. She hopped onto him, her legs encircling his waist, and sang in his ear, "Sweeps, I love you."

"Sa Ra Wa."

"Huh?"

"Sa Ra Wa. It means—shoot—I don't know what it means."

"Come be with us," Shadow said.

"I've got to—"

"No, you don't." Her legs tightened. "Don't be so responsible." She slid off him.

He let her lead him back through hundreds of people to where

Angelo sat holding a single jonquil someone had given him. Usually, his attempts to be cool made Sweeps imagine that pointed collar stays were poking into Angelo's neck. Today, however, Sweeps kept his attention on the flower and waved good-naturedly to Angelo.

Up on the stage, Tim Leary was talking. Over one ear he wore a white carnation with such sartorial correctness that it seemed part of a military uniform. His erect posture was enhanced by a lei of flowers and a string of beads around his neck.

Although the three of them were too far from the stage to hear much of what Leary was saying, the crowd closer in seemed appreciative. Murmurs of general agreement rippled over the meadow. They heard, "The only way out is in. . . . The only real revolution is the human one. . . . Your DNA . . .never . . . loves you. . . loves you. . . . Turn on."

"Too late, man!" shouted a man in front of them. "Did it already."

"Tune in," Leary said.

The crowd whooped and cheered.

"Drop out," he concluded, lifting his hands over his head like a politician celebrating victory.

Near Sweeps, Shadow and Angelo, five congo drummers started up, drowning out Leary. More and more people began to dance around the drummers. Angelo strained to hear Leary's words. Sweeps watched the dancers' feet trampling the grass. Shadow felt the drums pounding inside her. She started to get up, but Angelo's hand on her arm held her back. Her bare feet arched. She beat time with one heel.

The drummers formed a semicircle. A man whirled, and a space opened up. The man wore white drawstring pants and a loose flowered shirt; a single long strand of tiny glass beads swung round his neck, and his hair flowed halfway down his back. He was carrying what looked like two feedbags of heavy canvas with covers of silky sea green fabric. He was pulling small objects out of the bags and giving them to children. He danced away from the drummers, a long zigzag ramble, passing near the three of them twice in elliptical orbits. On his third pass, Shadow called to him, "Who are you?"

"The Candy Man. Anyone who needs sweetness gets sweetness."

She made a little cup of her hands. "You got a sweet for me?"

Still dancing, he flipped his hair back over his shoulder. "You're sweet enough already."

"Never, never, never."

"Right answer. For that, a sweet for each."

He dug into a bag, and put a candy into Shadow's mouth. From the other one he took two wrapped candies. "Be-In beauties. Greens are the best." Angelo unwrapped his and put the bright, shining green ball in his mouth. Sweeps put his in his pocket.

The Candy Man locked eyes with Shadow. Then, his hair flying, he danced away. "Greens—the best—in the universe!" Shadow blew him a kiss. He grabbed for it and stuffed it into one of his bags before disappearing into the crowd.

"God, I like today!" Sweeps said, resting back on his elbows. "This is the way people should be."

Angelo sucked his candy. "Hard to remember there's a war on."

"There's always a war going on," Sweeps said. "The thing that I'm getting, right now, right here, is there's a lot of peace coming on."

Angelo bit down hard on his candy. He chewed angrily, wondering what his father would say to this whole event. His mother's response was obvious. Her nose would curl, and she'd say, "Disgusting—indecent!" exactly as she did when she found the snail he'd put in her salad when he was nine. He looked at Sweeps, who met his gaze benignly.

"Sa Ra Wa, Buddha," Sweeps said. "Sa Ra Wa, Buddha."

"Am I supposed to know what you said?"

"He's just teasing you," Shadow said.

"Wa, Wa, Wa, Woolworth's!" Angelo said.

A band moved to the front of the stage and began to rearrange the sound pickups. On the apron, where he'd been since the first speech of the day, Suzuki-roshi, formally dressed in his Zen robes, sat Zazen as patiently as a stone sits in a river. He held a narcissus in his left hand. Below him, blanketing the meadow, thousands of souls rode their own waves of excitement. From his own roshi, he'd learned that tranquility was not a virtue but a necessity. He repeated the maxims he used to quiet himself:

Things take as long as they take.

Sit inside yourself.

Offer the teachings to any who come.

Make no distinctions.

A hard set of commandments. He strove not to sit in judgment, but just to sit. He attended to the speaker's words on his in-breath, the crowd's responses on his out-breath, music on the in-breath, dancing on the out-breath.

"We're in a liberation struggle—liberation for the whole planet," roared the amplified voice of a poet.

In-breath. Out-breath. "We are seeds of God ready to explode into flowers."

In-breath. Out-breath. Many of these people are my friends, Suzuki-roshi thought. In-breath. Ginsberg, the Jew, dresses like a Hindu. Out-breath. He loves their flamboyant gods and their pansexuality.

A sexual memory of the roshi's own hopped onto the meadow of his mind; another part, like a hawk, swooped down on it. In-breath. Oh Professor Leary—so little understanding, but such a great heart. Out-breath. He looked closely at the narcissus. In-breath. Beautiful one! No preferences. You live without concerns. He bowed with and to the flower.

In-breath, out-breath.

Jerry Rubin spoke against the war, about the killings in Vietnam, the moral right to fight the government and the necessity for active resistance. A small group sitting near the stage applauded, but for most of the people in the meadow he seemed out of place, unaware of the accepting mindset floating over the park. Expert at tuning out what didn't interest them, people withdrew into their own private reveries until Jerry finished. The muted hand-clapping at the end of his talk was more "Thank you for finishing" than "Thank you for what you said."

People began to dance. The Grateful Dead's pulsating music filled the meadow. Most of the crowd had listened to the speeches with goodwill, but not with the excitement that now lifted them to their feet. Thousands of tabs of Hawksmith acid had been distributed. White Lightning, in a green silk top and cutoffs, had, like other friends of Hawksmith's, dropped blue pills on strangers and friends until the leather bag tied to her wrist was empty.

Now, as more and more bodies became attuned to their own cellular rhythms, people let go of everything but sound. Pounding drums reverberated directly on bare flesh; music flowed in through a million open pores. Moonflower was in the center of a circle swaying and turning. At the edge of the stage, Jerry Rubin and the group of men who had come with him to bring Berkeley's radical political message to the psychedelic masses watched the cheerful revels with confusion.

Sweeps felt drawn to the bandstand before the music started. When the Dead began to play, he started to dance, until he saw Suzuki-roshi sitting. Then he too sat, trying to imitate the older man's upright posture.

On stage, Mickey Hart and Jerry Garcia led each other in and out of the musical cathedral they'd erected. Shadow felt herself break free, propelled by sound into pure spirit. Rocking back and forth, still hugging her knees, she looked over at Angelo. From her other side, hands touched hers, and lips kissed her cheek. She turned. "Maya!"

Dressed in matching rainbow shirts, the whole God Squad pressed in around her. "You're all here!" Shadow squealed.

"Did you ever doubt us?" Maya teased, stroking Shadow's hair.

"Gosh. I—"

"We've been watching over you."

"That's so cool!" Shadow said, holding her hands out as they all reached out for her.

"Glad you're with him," Maya said. She looked into Angelo's eyes. "We're her guardians from the stars."

"Glad to meet you," Angelo said, without conviction.

"Tell me what's happening," Shadow said.

"We're here to play," Maya said.

"And to touch in with you—for luck," Trevor added.

"There?" Shadow asked, pointing to the stage.

"Well, no," Maya said. "The poster said 'all the bands' so we knew they meant us even if they forgot our invite. We've set up near the merry-go-round. Come to hear us." She glanced at Angelo. "Or don't. Our teacher said that you will always be part of our family. We'll come back to get you when it's right."

"I'll be ready," said Shadow, hugging Maya.

Shadow waved at them until they disappeared into the trees. "They're the ones who took care of me in Santa Cruz."

Angelo nodded, barely aware of what she'd said. The band's music and the people surrounding them made him uneasy. When the God Squad had been so close he'd felt trapped. The police, half-hidden and silent on their horses, seemed menacing. The children screaming with pleasure, pushing and pulling one another, seemed almost feral. Reflections from earrings, bracelets, even from beads of sweat on people's arms and shoulders were so bright he had to close his eyes.

Shadow lay down and put her head in his lap. He looked at her and smiled weakly. When she smiled back, the excessive whiteness of her teeth hurt his eyes.

"You all right?"

"Yeah. A little cold, maybe," he said.

She stared up at his pale face and at his pupils—large, dark and featureless. She pulled his head down closer. He felt her breath, unpleasantly warm across his nose.

"Are you stoned?" Her voice sounded far away.

He was staring at a Hell's Angel who sat a few feet down the slope, so hairy that he seemed to have black wool patches on his chest, hair epaulets on each shoulder. He'll beat the shit out of me, he thought, if I look at him the wrong way. The Angel looked up the hill. Angelo stared at his own feet. He pulled away from Shadow, who lay back on the grass watching him.

"You're not okay, are you," she said, pronouncing each word carefully.

"I'm fine." He shivered. "Just a little—it's nothing."

"You look stoney as all get out."

"I'm fine! Been sitting too long, that's all. I'll—up." Unable to get his legs to uncross, he used both hands to lift one knee away from the other. Then, rolling onto hands and knees, he tried to stand. He fell over and lay there, his arms and legs bent. Shadow hauled him to his feet.

She took his face in her hands and pulled it close to hers. "We're leaving right now, together."

He nodded, holding onto her for support. She would take him out of this place before the Angel pummeled him, before the police, billy clubs swinging, rode him down. He didn't want to be beaten. He stifled the sobs he felt in his chest. Shadow squeezed both his hands, then let them go. They fell to his sides.

"Just keep your feet going," she said. "I'm leading you home."

"My home is on South River Road in Stamford, Connecticut," he said, staying as close to her as he could.

CHAPTER 24

The second cage

I do not doubt that
dangerous substances such as LSD
cause us to transcend habitual ways of experiencing.
But transcending in itself is not enough.

S. I. Hayakawa

IN WASHINGTON THE WEATHER WAS CHILL, gray and overcast. Langwater was sitting in a Pentagon office with no name on the door.

"Mister Langwater."

Langwater became wary whenever his superior addressed him as "Mister." The colonel behind the desk put down a tattered manila file bulging with papers and leaned back in his chair.

"You advocate that we not only advance funds to repair the damages sustained at the San Francisco facility, but that we also expand the research. Your audacity surprises me."

"If you'll allow me to clarify—"

The look on the other's face allowed for no interruptions. "Your report is clear. You've tried to put a good face on it, but this harebrained scheme seems to have finally fallen on its face. I will add my own evaluation before I pass it up the line." The official scraped a match along the bottom of his shoe. He sucked the match flame deep into his pipe.

"Sir, this work proves we have new ways to break agents open—far superior to physical torture. LSD-25 drives people out of their minds, but only temporarily. It leaves no trace, not a hint of its having been given."

"Pardon my French, Doctor Langwater, but who gives a flying fuck about a commie's mental health?" A quick tight smile passed under his mustache. A ring of smoke floated toward Langwater's right ear.

"But sir, since this madness doesn't last, we tell them, 'We'll do it to you again—only this time you won't recover.' Fear is a sharper probe than pain can ever be."

"Go on, Langwater."

"Fear holds them in our hands like a pin through a beetle."

The officer laced his fingers together, one after another. "Years ago, doctor, I conducted some experiments. We put a dog in a cage and shocked him—severely. Let him jump into a second cage to escape. Then we electrified the second cage as well. After a while, our dogs stopped jumping, just cowered and whimpered. Dogs died in the first cage rather than jump."

Langwater tried to look impressed. "Interesting, sir. You seem to have been ahead of me."

"It worked with monkeys as well."

"Impressive, sir."

The officer gazed out the window. "Perhaps you see where I'm heading?"

"Well, sir, I'm not sure," Langwater said, wrinkling his brow in what he hoped looked like perplexity. "You're still ahead of me." He pretended to ponder for a moment, then raised his eyebrows. "Combine our studies?"

"Consider it, doctor. Might save you and your project from the circular file." The officer struck another match and turned his attention to relighting his pipe. "Why don't you redo the report? Have it back to me by the end of the week."

"Certainly, sir."

Another smoke ring rolled across the desk. Langwater pushed his hand through it to retrieve his report.

After Langwater left, the colonel leaned back, put his hands behind his head and blew smoke rings. Later, he added a note to Langwater's file. "Remains firmly fixated on his own navel, but may be goaded into something productive by a threat to his pet project. Managed to lead him to a place that should open a new avenue of research within the scope of his limited vision."

"Whatever owl shit Langwater puts together, make it look fundable," he told his junior officer the next day.

"Yes, sir. You're letting him go ahead, then?"

"Not sure. Upstairs is nervous. All the drug projects are on thin ice."

"Anything new?"

"A veiled threat from our inspector general. He told the press he was looking at every study to be sure all the work was ethical. As if the fucking commies are playing parlor games." The officer sucked on his pipe. "A shame my work didn't get the full test." A thin trail of smoke drifted toward the ceiling. "Might get Langwater to jump into the second cage." He blew a perfect ring.

"Sir?"

"Forget it. Check over the little weasel's report and highlight what he's changed before you pass it by me."

"Will do, sir."

CHAPTER 25

Doing wonderfully

The fundamental reason
for taking psychedelics
is for the experiences
they produce.

Bernard Aaronson, Ph.D., and Humphry Osmond, M.D.

ANGELO FOLLOWED SHADOW up Oak Street obediently, like a well-trained sheep dog. He found every reflecting surface painful to look at. To avoid the glare, he stared at Shadow's hair. Every strand continued to undulate even when she stood still. Could hair communicate? Could he have a relationship with it even when she was asleep? He touched his own hair, then the stubble on his chin. Signs he'd seen on a road in Illinois two summers ago rolled across his mind.

To kiss
a mug
that's like a cactus
takes more nerve
than it does practice.
Burma Shave.

Shadow's voice broke through his reverie. "Pay attention! We're crossing the street. Hold on to me and just keep walking. . . walk, walk, walk. It's only a few more blocks."

Getting from the curb to the street didn't look easy. It seemed so high. Angelo leapt off with both feet and landed at the edge of an oily puddle. He stopped, worrying that he'd hurt the water. Prodded by Shadow, he moved on. Even holding on to her, he almost fell when the pavement suddenly became spongy.

"The street's too soft," he said.

"Sure, sure." She gripped his fingers and thought about the kid who had come into the store last week, high on something. Kept wanting to punch the windows. Said his hand could go through the glass just like light did. He showed her his fist. "It's made of light," he said. "We're all made of light."

"I'm going to count our steps," Shadow said. "You count with me. One, two, three, four. One, two, three, four."

Angelo struggled to pay attention. Someone was marching ahead of him. Angelo realized it was his father, and in front of him, his grandfather. Beyond them other men were marching. He tried to look behind him, but he couldn't turn his head.

Shadow's voice continued. "One, two, three, four."

Dry dust raised by the marching feet settled on his boots and the legs of his combat fatigues. They had been marching as long as he could remember. This was the reality, everything else a dream. "Hey, Dad!" he called. His father didn't turn around. The dusty road vanished. He was walking stiff-legged up Clayton, Shadow guiding him.

"I'm back," he said.

"You sure?" She let go of his hand.

"Uh-huh." He straightened up and, feeling magnificent and robust, walked into the house, striding straight up the stairs to Shadow's room.

He lay down on her mattress. Once off his feet, however, his confidence left him. His teeth began to chatter.

"I'll get you a blanket," she said, and was gone.

"I'm stoned. I'm really stoned!" he said to the ceiling. That candy! The green one. He remembered mint flavor. Not for her, for me.

He squatted on his haunches by the side of the road with the rest of the marchers. The sun was painfully hot. Dust caked his lips. He didn't even try to lick it off. The barren road stretched ahead to a brown, featureless horizon.

Shadow wasn't coming back. Sweeps would find him here. He'd throw Angelo out. Shadow told me to lie here, he'd say. But Sweeps wouldn't care. Oh, please, please come back. God, bring her back.

He saw a flash of color on the bedside table. There, taped to one edge, was a diffraction grating. Gazing at it, he found himself engulfed in a rainbow haze. Vast moving waves of rainbow on every side. And you never even opened the box, part of his mind mocked. The waves of color moved faster. He tried to slow them down. Failed. He felt unsteady and covered his eyes. The rainbows smudged into a muddy brown.

Hearing a noise, he raised his head. When Angelo saw Shadow return through the open door, he burst into loud sobs.

"Here," she said, putting an olive green army-issue blanket over him. "I'm here—really here. Long as you want." She stroked his face. "I'll put on some music."

Feigning cheerfulness, he asked, "Hey, I'm not going to die, am I?"

"Probably not. But if you do, it's all right. It's just a feeling."

He recalled the story of the man who fell off the Empire State Building, saying, as he passed the fiftieth floor, "So far, so good." Angelo laughed. Life was like that. You start to fall at birth. Never know when the pavement is coming up. If you die, well. . . go with the feeling. He could die, then!

His thoughts came faster and faster, flowed through him and hurtled past. He reached for one, but it slipped away like mercury and sped on, pushed by those behind it. Help! he thought. But he couldn't keep "help" any longer than any other thought.

With every ounce of his strength, he paddled the battered Lake Thorson Boys Camp canoe ("Boys become men on the waters of Lake Thorson," his mind recited). The thoughts stayed well ahead of him, however, far downstream. Seized with a sudden shrewdness, he turned the canoe around. Sure enough, another flotilla of thoughts were floating down the river. Were they his? If not, whose? He shuddered.

He stood before rows of iron cages—all his thoughts captured. He tried to open one, but he had no key. He pulled on another door, grunting with the effort. It was rusted shut. A thought rushed against the bars. "Let go," it said. He let go. The door swung open. Thoughts flew past him like flocks of birds.

Who was he? No answer. His body? A windup toy. Memories flew away. Thinking remained. I think, therefore, I am. Cogito. Cogito. Cogito! Not dead after all!

Shadow's shoulder blades moved under her sweater as she flipped through a stack of records.

"I am not me, you know," he said, hoisting himself up on one elbow.

"I'm not you, either," she said. "Or me."

"How do you know?" he asked.

"LSD helped," she said, her voice bright as wind chimes. "I've tripped a few times."

"Am I on LSD?"

She smiled. "Is the Pope Catholic?"

He became confused. Actually many popes had not been Catholic, even in a spiritual sense. Some had been violent, corrupt, avaricious men. Alexander VI had slept with his own daughter, Lucrezia Borgia, and probably had sex with horses, and he wasn't the worst of them. He could hear Luther declaim, "Hearest Thou, O Pope, not most holy of men but most sinful. Oh that God from Heaven would soon destroy thy throne, and sink it in the abyss of Hell!"

Angelo was standing near four huge men in red velvet robes. They held ornate silver miters. Suddenly they turned toward him. He tried to run away but his feet took root. As his body turned to wood, their miters became silver axes.

"Help!" he croaked. Shadow didn't seem to hear. "Help," he said again. The popes came closer.

CHAPTER 26

Angelo set free

The Glory of Him
... glows ever more bright
In that heaven
which most allows his light.

Dante, *Paradiso*, Canto I

T HE GOD SQUAD played to a small group of adults and children
on the sparse lawn near the merry-go-round. Maya held several
small children's hands as she sang:

> *Welcome to this drama*
> *to find out who you are.*
> *Welcome to this universe,*
> *in which you are the star.*

She danced with the children as the band repeated the chorus.

In his office, Bear fumed over Washington's critique of his monthly ex-
pense reports. For the fourth straight month, the Agency's internal audi-

tor asked for a detailed justification of the same items he'd explained three times already.

The Grateful Dead, having finished their second set, were packing up their instruments. The crowd pleaded for yet one more encore. Jerry Garcia picked up the last live mike. "Hey, everybody. This is only the beginning. We're just the warm-up band for the music going on inside you."

White Lightning was sandwiched between two men, one white, one black. Dear Abby, she thought, looking from one to the other. I am at a large informal social gathering sitting between two drug dealers. I am turned on to both of them, and they to me. What is the best way to keep both their affections? If I tell one I intend to leave with the other, the one left behind might do something ugly. Is there a correct way so I do not get beaten up or bring down the pigs on us all? Sincerely, Double-barrelled in San Francisco.

She moved a hand off the inside of her thigh, sighed deeply, and hoped something would resolve the situation.

Across her bedroom, Shadow saw Angelo's eyes frozen with fear. She reached out and touched his shoulder. "Whatever you're feeling, let it go."

The popes' axe-miters withdrew, shrinking until they vanished from sight. "Thank you," Angelo said weakly.

Shadow placed a record on the shaft of the record player. Angelo watched the turntable begin to rotate. The record teetered, then dropped with a smack onto the mat. The tone arm raised itself, poised above the outer edge, then dove gracefully down, setting the needle into the spiral-in groove.

"Close your eyes and listen," Shadow said.

Processions of red and black checkers filled Angelo's mind, swaying, then parading, then flying by. Waves of color spread across vast spaces. A vibrating G-major chord from a steel guitar string blew the colors away, leaving a pearly surface. The hard-edged nasal twang of Bob Dylan's voice etched designs across it. As Dylan sang "Hey, Mister Tambourine Man," the shimmering surface broke into fragments.

"Jingle jangle." Angelo saw and heard staffs of silver bells, their tones chording in long even rows. "You have no one to meet—" Angelo tasted loneliness, brackish and metallic on his tongue. Shadow was far away. He was alone. Everyone is always alone. Everyone. Always. Always. Everyone.

He couldn't feel his body. Was he breathing? It didn't seem important. "I'm ready to fade." Fade—fade—fade—echoed inside him. Aha! This, then, was death. Nothing to lose, nothing to fear.

Angelo moved through a featureless darkness. The sorrow of separation surged through him. He was the earth. He felt the sun's pull. He yearned to move closer. But then a mist cleared in his mind and he saw his urge was a wish to die. To join the sun, to give in to her attraction, was to be destroyed.

"The earth," Angelo said, trying to squeeze the enormity of his experience into words, "wants to be free."

Shadow seemed to understand. "Stay with it."

Dylan's harmonica blew insistently. Angelo saw the ceiling open, revealing huge rings of clouds. He rose toward them.

Oh God, this time he was dying! Soaring through the rings, they shifted from brilliant white to pale white, then darker and darker until there was no white left at all.

Death might be, after all, the least interesting state. He found himself amused at the thought—and at still being able to think. After death, is there still thought? How long would it continue? He was falling toward a pinpoint of light. He knew, without knowing how he knew, that he would fall forever. This was his true state—to fall eternally toward the light.

Might he fall up? Immediately he felt himself stretched as thin as a soap bubble. He rose. As he did, he sensed other presences; he was one of many, one of multitudes! He was one-who-joined-together. Not a person, not a planet. Humbled by having forgotten this.

Peals of laughter fanned out like rings of water on a pond. Alone? Alone? Alone? It was an idea beyond comic. There could no more be aloneness than there could be death.

Suddenly a wave of darkness engulfed him. No, please. No more death, no more darkness. Even as he cried out, the dark universe began to fill with light. Far ahead he saw a glowing human form. He felt its love. It was Christ! Desperately, gratefully Angelo flew toward him.

Then empty space.

Christ was no longer there, but the light and the love remained. When he looked back, he saw steel corner brackets, plywood and pine framing. Christ was no more than a billboard, a highway sign between the stars! A voice sang, "Drop-kick me, Jesus, through the goal posts of life." Convulsed with laughter, Angelo turned back toward the light. He was going home.

When she heard Angelo laugh, Shadow stretched out and relaxed.

Angelo merged into the light and sang with the other voices. These beings interpenetrated Angelo, blending harmoniously yet retaining their identities. The shared existence was blissful. Gleefully, they sang of the hide-and-seek Angelo had played, losing and finding himself.

The song and the singers made a vast ring. Its dark formless center attracted Angelo. He flowed forward to fill it. The center resisted his entry. He grew in volume, plunging more of himself toward the blackness. The voices fell away. More radiant than a hundred suns, he arrayed himself against the darkness. The darkness tore holes in him. Joyfully he filled them with light. The darkness writhed in his grasp.

"In opposing, you give me form," it said. The darkness spread and covered him. "You are alone, and I am everywhere."

In tears, Angelo looked over at Shadow. She was now sitting in a half-lotus posture, her eyes closed, her breathing regular. "I lost it all," he said.

Shadow opened her eyes. "Maybe." Bright light emanated from her body. Ranks of angelic beings spun around her. The medieval images in Doré's etchings—reminders! Others had seen and remembered. In Shadow's voice he heard the echo of the joy.

"I'm you. I'm so much. I—" he said.

"I know," she said.

Did she really know the terrible, unending constriction and ignorance of this life? Imprisoned in a body, unable to touch the inner core of any other person and terrified of death?

He blinked. Glory enveloped him.

"Forgot so soon?" she teased.

"So close," he whispered. "Is it always this close?"

"Always. Always and forever. Like this." Shadow held her fingers very close together. "But we forget." She snapped her fingers. "Then, poof—we remember. It's a game." She put her finger across his lips. "No more words."

"I'm God," he said into her fingers.

"Me, too."

She put her other hand over his eyes; its coolness calmed him. Infinity in a grain of sand, he thought. Of course—obvious, obvious.

He recalled his physics professor, Dr. Malcolm Tambert, slamming his hand onto the podium, his distended belly shaking. "Nothing but dancing atoms, gentlemen! No-things hitting other no-things. You are little else but atoms dancing." Dr. Tambert had been in a German prison camp during World War II. He said that recalling the laws of physics every day kept him sane. "The laws of e-tern-it-y, gentlemen, the always and forevers."

Angelo saw Bear at his desk, a beer can near his hand. "No-things hitting no-things," Dr. Tambert said. Angelo watched the cloud of dancing atoms that were Bear's hand encircle the dancing atoms of the beer can.

In a single breath, Angelo became aware of the equality of all things.

He looked at Shadow, saw her head on her neck on her body, her legs crossed under her torso, and understood cubism. He saw her sitting on the bed, the mattress dipping slightly where her weight had compressed the springs, and understood Platinous. He saw the window and in knowing that the view outside was the view inside, understood the non-dualistic nature of the perceived world.

Is part of the game to pretend you're not God? Jesus no more than a cardboard cutout on the route to Heaven? Buddha, Moses, Zeus—more cutouts? Burma Shave slogans on the roads to Paradise?

Be a noble, not a knave,
Caesar uses Burma Shave.

God tells us how we must behave,
Jesus uses Burma Shave.

Nobody knows de stubble I've seen.
Glory, glory, hallelujah.

God loves to cover and uncover himself. He is like a kitten playing with yarn. Finding himself, he applauds, then hides again. Everything is God—every damn thing!

Tears flowed down Angelo's face. "Is there anything but God-hide and God-seek?"

Shadow rubbed her eyes and said, "I have an apple for you."

God wants God to have an apple. He hesitated. An apple? God sent them out of Eden to play hide-and-be-sought. God never stops playing. God's little slithering pal gave them a drugged apple. That was the clue. Once aware of the knowledge you could never go back to what you'd been. Ignorance is not bliss, knowledge is. The secret protects itself.

Angelo gazed at the apple on the plate. It was luminous; the gentle tilt of the stem asked him to touch it. He did and the fruit parted, falling into two pieces. He picked one up. His eyes caressed it. He savored the line of skin, the white flesh glistening with jewels of juice, the core and the exposed seed. Such complex perfection. The curve of its skin let the light slide over its glossy surface. This apple came from the tree of knowledge as did every other apple. The knowledge that he was hungry, and that he was holding food, felt as if the gift and the giver had become a single being.

As he bit into the apple, he became aware of the perfection of what he was doing. The piece of apple in his mouth was exactly the right size. It touched his tongue and the roof and the sides of his mouth precisely where it should. His eyes filled with tears of pleasure.

"You okay?" Shadow said, and leaned toward him.

"Oh, yes. I'm one der full." The words flowed out around the apple bits in his mouth, each sound equally flawless. "Infinity in a grain of sand."

"Is there sand on it?" Shadow moved to take the apple.

"No, no. It's perfect." He chewed, reveling in the harmony of his lips, tongue and teeth working together.

"You're dripping," she said, and kissed a corner of his mouth.

Was it still perfect? It was. Everything was exactly as it should be. The juice, her kiss. How could anything be other than it was? Everything had to be perfect! He lay down again.

Christ died for our sins. Why did he bother? Wasn't it perfect to suffer? He died to remind us. Of course—Re-Member. Drilled into him—all those Sundays he never understood.

Angelo walked along a dusty street, jostled by the excited crowd. He had to find Jesus, tell him not to do it. Sin didn't exist, only perfection and forgetfulness. Nothing to forgive. Angelo pushed his way to the front. Jesus was already on the cross. Their eyes met.

He saw that Christ forgave him; he forgave everyone. For they know not that they have forgotten. Angelo saw the darkness. Christ falling into the hands of the darkness—forgetting, suffering.

"Forgetting is the only sin," he said.

Shadow nestled close to him. "So, don't forget."

"I can't help it."

"Then maybe it's not a sin."

He pondered her idea. "But it is a problem."

"Problem, problems, always problems." She rubbed her face into his neck.

"Do you ever forget?" he asked.

"Sure, but sometimes, when I remember—" She sat up, then straddled him and pinned his arms down against the blanket. "Oh boy! When I do, it's a total gas!"

Angelo lay on his back, chained to the floor with heavy iron shackles on his wrists and ankles. Guards entered his cell. One kicked him in the side. The other slammed his boot into Angelo's jaw. He grunted from the pain. Then—he remembered. The chains fell away. He clanged his wrist irons together. The clanging became rows of singing angels. His bracelets were silver—diamonds—flowers, and were gone. He heard the teasing laughter.

Shadow brushed her hair back and forth over his face.

"I remembered," he said, grinning up at her.

"Whoopee!" she said, and kept on brushing.

He recalled how Christ had looked at him. Christ died to remind us. Apples grow to remind us. Shadow's hair reminds me. Everywhere, reminders to redeem ourselves.

He reached up to hug Shadow. She let herself be captured in his arms.

He heard the music again.

CHAPTER 27

The sun sets
even on the finest of days

Pure and spontaneous pleasures
are patches of Godlight
in the woods of our experience.

C. S. Lewis

THE WESTERN EDGE of Golden Gate Park extends to the sea. Below Murphy's Windmill and the tulip garden, a sandy margin cut by the Great Highway reemerges as low dunes descend to the water. That evening, thousands of bare and sandaled feet covered the road, stitching the park and beach together. Closely packed people swayed, holding each others' waists and shoulders. As the sun began to pierce the waters of the Pacific, the crowd chanted exuberantly, "Lord of Light," as if God were truly listening. They chanted, "Help us make this world a paradise!" Half-asleep children, slumped over their parents' shoulders, murmured the words. Older people, their joints creaking and clicking under stretched tired muscles, joined in. Everyone chanted their aspirations, their renewed determination to love one another. Members of a dozen bands wove their voices into the fabric, sustaining and enriching the musical tapestry. The chant became a drum, beating on the skin of the earth.

Allen Ginsberg, standing knee-deep in the surf, felt forgiven, blessed and renewed. Waves of the chant passed through him. This time, he prayed, let all of humanity be your chosen people!

Inside the park, the police rode their horses back to the stables. "Damnedest bunch I've ever seen," the captain said. "More noise, more nudity, more goddamned dope than I've ever seen. But, you know, the bastards left the place clean."

"Yeah. The Kike in the white pants says 'Leave no traces' and those shit-eaters pick it all up," said an officer riding close to the captain. "I'd like to have hippies do the trash every day."

"Why don't we give 'em shovels and little bags and turn 'em loose in the zoo?" said another. Laughing, they urged their horses through the gathering darkness.

The sun hovered, as if hesitating to enter the sea. A light washed over the singing crowd. On the dunes stood a few Hell's Angels, not chanting, but unable or unwilling to leave. At the edge of the road Father O'Malley belted out the chant as if he had sung the sun down every evening of his life. He was keenly aware that the woman leaning back on him wore no bra. He held on to her, excited by her every movement. He envisioned acts he'd pored over in the sex manuals he'd confiscated from Roxbury teenagers. His pleasure was heightened by the remoteness of the possibilities. Inadvertently practicing karma yoga, chanting Sanskrit and meditating on the setting sun, his face was almost beatific.

Held from behind by Father O'Malley's arms, acutely aware of the warmth of his body, Moonflower chanted. The rough weave of her top rubbed against her nipples. Twice she'd moved so his hands would touch her breasts; both times he'd jerked away. She leaned back against his chest. What the hell, this guy kept moving his hands near her breasts, but sure seemed scared. What was his problem? Tits too big? Not big enough? Not likely. He sang good. Really good. Part of a band? Not with those scaredy-cat hands. Maybe a pansy band. Moonflower and the Pansies. No good. Sounds like a troop of effeminate gardeners.

She raised her pitch a third and sang harmony. Father O'Mally joined her, note for note. She snuggled back into him. Whooee! This small-pricked puppy can really sing! She chanted louder. He stiffened and went silent. His hands slid down to her waist. She lowered her voice and sweetened it. His tenor resumed. His hands returned to her chest.

A hundred yards down the road, White Lightning, flanked by the two drug dealers, continued to delay what she now sensed was an inevitable confrontation. But, as the sun touched the water, the dealer on her right was approached by a heavyset man in worn leathers, his matted beard and hair flecked with reddish dust. They spoke together, too quietly for her to hear.

Then the dealer's mustache rubbed her cheek. "Sweetie, a bunch of Detroit bikers." His tongue dipped in and out of her ear. "They wanta load up and roll out." She made a little yipping noise, and momentarily lost the chant.

"I'm their man. I'm outta here." He bit her ear.

White Lightning dipped her chin to hide her smile. The dealer let her go and began to push his way through the crowd, the dusty biker in his wake. White Lightning leaned into the other dealer's shoulder and slipped an arm around his waist.

Toss a Hindu God a few heartfelt chants, she thought, and he saves your ass. She put a hand over the one grasping her hip. Hey God! You with the three heads and fucking fifty arms—you're A-okay with me. She kissed the dealer's cheek with a smack.

The sun completed its descent with unfailing grace and slowly penetrated the water. It became a half-circle that shrank until only a sliver of light remained. The ascending rows of faces, from the water's edge up the dunes, across the road and onto the grass, seemed transfixed. Jets of pink streamed up from the horizon, spotlighting a few high clouds. The clear sky turned rose. The clouds darkened, the sky turned violet, the water flashed silver. Then the sea was infused with royal purple deepening to the color of dark wine. The tops of the waves turned into gray lines on black slate.

The sun took a final, infinitesimal bow and dove into the sea. Everyone fell silent. Then, like spirits that vanish at cock's crow, they left without speaking. Within minutes the small waves, each preceded by a hand of white foam, scudded up the beach, slapped softly on the sand and smoothed away the last of their footprints.

CHAPTER 28

It's all love

There are hundreds of ways
to kneel and kiss the ground.

Rumi

A HALF-HOUR PASSED. Angelo had been silent for so long that Shadow began to fidget.

"It's all love," he said.

She nodded vigorously.

"I love you," he said softly.

"I like that you said it, but you're too stoned to mean it."

"No, I'm not."

"Are so."

She rolled away from him and took a small oblong mirror from her bedside table. "Just look."

Lying on his back, he held it up with both hands. A portion of his face looked down at him. He pulled the mirror closer. "Eyes big as fruit pies. Still drugged, huh?"

"Stoned! Super stoned."

Angelo tried to hand her the mirror.

Shadow pushed it back. "Keep looking."

He stared. The lines between his eyes grew more pronounced, the pores on his nose grew larger, his hair was thinning and had receded. A much older Angelo looked back at him. He glanced over at Shadow. "That's me?" She pointed back to the mirror.

He saw himself again. But almost immediately, the skin around his eyes turned dark. He saw a man with deep lines around his mouth wearing a gray, frayed turban. The man melted into a child with a pock-marked face and stringy black hair plastered across a low forehead. He stared into a woman's face, her eyes moist, her gaze loving and serene. She metamorphosed into a woman with a face so bloated even her eyes were buried in folds of flesh. Then her skin discolored and fell away, exposing her skull. The skull turned yellow and crumbled. He slapped the mirror down.

"Who are all those people?" he asked.

"Who'd they look like?"

He was silent for a moment. "Like me?"

"Well?"

Did she know what he'd seen? Impossible. They seemed so disconnected from one another. "Everything is connected," his mind sang. He'd forgotten. The angels passed through him.

"Shadow. Please remember for me: Don't hold on! It's real important."

"Will do."

"Thanks." He sat up trembling. He covered the mirror with one hand and shook his head. "I don't understand all this."

She grinned. "I don't really understand anything much, but the world seems to work okay anyway."

"I'm so glad I'm with you," he said.

"You're so beautiful right now! Yum, yum. I could make love with you, for a hundred years." Shadow wriggled with pleasure.

Angelo flopped back down on the mattress and stared at the ceiling.

"If this is Heaven, it's got queer rules," he said.

"It is Heaven, and it does have queer rules!"

They laughed. He took her hand.

"You know about the mirror?"

"Sweeps showed me."

"Were you stoned?"

"Yeah."

He tilted the mirror back up. His face looked normal. He looked closer, saw blond stubble on one side of his face; the other was satin-smooth. Even the scar he'd gotten playing field hockey his freshman year was gone. The first side now had a full blond-brown beard. One eyebrow was larger and darker than the other. He turned away from the mirror. "Help," he said.

"Remember, 'Don't hold on,'" Shadow said, mimicking Angelo's tone of voice.

"Remember," he repeated. Remember what? What did he want so much to remember?

He handed her the mirror. She put it back on the table and turned to him, her chin in her hands.

"You're starting to come down."

"I don't want to."

"It's one of the rules."

He looked at the window. It was dark outside. "What time is it?"

"Does it matter?"

"I guess not."

"When it starts to matter, you're down."

PART IV

CHAPTER 29

God kisses God

Any house in which you dwell
Does not need lamps

Shibli

A week later, Angelo sat at his desk rereading a letter from Dan.

I hear that San Francisco is hot shit. Bet you're
getting lots of chicks. Trade places with you any
time. Dad's store is a fucking drag. Everyone treats
me as if I'm the boss's son, and need to have everything explained twice. Well, big deal. I'm learning
how to run the place, but I wish I were back in
school. (Can't believe I just wrote that!)

Angelo stopped reading, folded the letter and absentmindedly rubbed it along his chin. Dan's nose was splotched with freckles, and topped by thick glasses that enlarged his hazel eyes. Angelo recalled how often Dan had stood at the bottom of the stairwell of Fraser Hall, a plain white T-shirt and khaki shorts hanging on his bony frame, yelling, "Emergency!

Emergency! Dan's out of beer."

He wrote back,

```
Dear Dan,
I've discovered that you and I are more than col-
lege friends, more than separate souls. The world
has become so beautiful and clear since I've experi-
enced the truth of things. I don't know how to begin
to write this, however, without freaking you out.
    Premise: Everyone is a piece of God.
    Conclusion: This includes me and you.
    Discussion: I checked all this out. A stranger
gave me a dose of LSD strong enough to melt down
everything stupid in me at once. It did.
    Follow me, if you can. Remember in Art History—
you were awake that morning? Doré's illustrations of
Dante's Paradiso, the rings of holy souls. And
Blake's flowing blending beings of light. They're
what I've experienced, what you and I are.
Wordsworth wrote about it. Bach composed it. I've
heard the music, felt the joy! All of it, Dan. All of
it close to me even now.
```

He imagined Dan trying to make sense of his words, passing this letter around to friends. None of them would understand. He tore the letter into eight neat pieces and dropped them, one by one, into the wastebasket beside his dresser.

Shadow looked up as Angelo appeared in the Trip Shop doorway. She stood back and shielded her eyes. "Wow! Aren't you radiant!"

"I'm flying."

"Without crashing?"

"If I do, I'll rise again." He stood beside her.

"You've got it," she said.

"How could I not get it?"

"Oh, people manage."

"I never even knew God—was," Angelo said.

Shadow took his hand and kissed his knuckles one by one.

Angelo stroked her hair. "I've tossed coins into the bowl at church, but I had no idea. It's an amazing story: Clean-cut, East Coast, uptight agnostic comes west. Falls in with drug-dealing angels."

"Creepy."

"Worse than you think. Flash! After divine intervention, same guy finds himself insanely devoted to angel disguised as dropout teen beauty."

"Same East Coast guy?"

"No, he left. Gone so far I can't even remember what he was like."

"I liked him," Shadow said, hugging him.

"Should you want him—" He picked her up off the floor and swung around. "I will find him and bring him to you." He put her down.

"You're going too fast for me."

He closed his eyes for a moment. "I just came by to tell you God is in love with you."

"Did he tell you to tell me?"

"Hey." He pulled her close and whispered, "The real truth, and it still shakes me up, is that I am God!"

She stood on her toes and kissed him.

"What was that for?"

She ran behind the counter. "God just kissed God, Mr. Smarty."

"You too?"

"What do you think I take drugs for—to burn my brains out? Now out of my way, or God'll push you out the door. I have to sort the bills that wonderful people—all of them God—have run up over the past two months."

"Am I the only one around here who didn't know?"

"Uncool as ever! Sweet one, you were an unenlightened square." She looked him up and down. "Now you're an enlightened one. But so cute. Yum."

He shook his head. "I don't get it."

She laughed and ducked under the counter.

"Wait! I do get it"

Shadow popped up like a jack-in-the-box and threw her arms open.

"One more kiss, and this piece of God, now humbled and contrite, will fly along his way." They kissed, and kissed again. "I'm so turned on, God better watch her step. Deity abduction may occur."

"Are you saying I'm seeing you tonight?"

"Unless I'm recalled to Heaven or the button molder melts me down for scrap."

"Goody!" She blew him a kiss and, opening her arms again, embraced the air between them. With a whoop, he bounded out of the shop.

That night, on his way to the Clayton house, he dropped a letter into the metal mailbox at the corner.

Dear Dan,

A lot is going on out here that is wonderful. Impossible to write what I feel. Come visit if you can. Don't believe the bad press about LSD. Lucy _is_ in the sky with diamonds. Listen to the Jefferson Airplane. Stay open. I care a lot about you.

CHAPTER 30

Angelo's run

All guns are good guns.
There are no bad guns.
I say the whole nation should be armed,
period.

Joe Foss, President, The National Rifle Association

WE BUSTED OUR BUTTS for you, man, to score that acid. Will you help us or won't you?" Nitrous Eddie bumped the table as he stood up, rattling the dishes left from dinner. Angelo twisted in his chair. He turned his plate round and round, staring fixedly at its center. Shadow and Moonflower's eyes met. The room was quiet.

"I'll try," Angelo said. He looked across the table at Sweeps. "But since we were robbed, it's not going to be easy."

Eddie snorted. "If it was easy, man, I'd score it myself." He walked out. Moonflower cleared the table and vanished into the kitchen. Shadow trailed after her. As Sweeps passed Angelo, he gave his shoulder a squeeze.

The tiny clicks sounded loud in Angelo's ear as the pins in the lock slid into place. He eased out the key and slowly opened the drawer. As he did so, a thin string attached to the back of it went taut, silently closing a switch. In Bear's room, a small bell sounded. Grunting as he made his way out of bed, Bear moved to his dresser. In the dark, he rumaged through the top drawer for his pistol. Pushing it through his sleeve as he put on his robe, he slipped into the hall. He glided to the head of the stairwell. A streetlight shining through a small high window lit the banister, but the ground floor was dark.

Twenty blocks away, Lupe de Vega was driving home. Stoked on his own heroin, he drove without haste, floating down block after dark quiet block, as free of joy as he was empty of anxiety.

He rarely came into the Haight. Most of its residents lacked the money for a sizable buy, and those with money preferred marijuana and psychedelics. Lupe only dealt high-quality hard drugs. He had started as a runner for older members of his family, carrying everything from nickel bags on up. Eventually he went on his own. As Vietnam heated up and his supply lines allowed him to maintain a steady stock of hard drugs, he no longer bothered selling marijuana. This evening, he'd bought three kilos of heroin from a soldier home on leave, a carrier for a senior officer who was a regular in Lupe's operation. The heroin came from Cambodian poppies, refined in Thailand—the refinery established, Lupe had been told, with CIA support, an irony that he appreciated as the war dragged on.

From the top of the stairs, Bear heard a doorknob turn. He went down one step. The stair creaked loudly. He heard someone race toward the kitchen. As he lumbered down the stairs, he fired once. The shot hit the hallway floor. He heard the back door of the house open.

"Stop, you bastard!" Bear roared.

The door slammed shut. Bear wheeled about, ran to the front door and flung it open. Across the street, he saw a figure running away.

Bear plunged down the steps. As the person rounded the corner onto Waller Street, he got off a second shot. The bullet pinged off a brick wall. He raced around the corner up toward Clayton, puffing and sweating. The street was deserted. He fired a shot into the air. Lights went on. Bear became aware of how he looked—barefoot, in his bathrobe and carrying a gun. Cursing, he scurried back to the house.

The second shot, although almost a block away, brought Easy to full alert. He pulled on his pants. When the third shot went off, he dropped to the floor. On hands and knees, staying well away from the windows, he crawled toward the stairs.

Crying and gasping, holding the box of LSD vials tight against his chest, Angelo could barely see. He ducked behind a car and scuttled past a few more doorways. When he heard the final shot, he burst head down into the street between two parked cars and headed for the Clayton house.

Had Lupe been on methedrine instead of heroin, he might have been able to swerve around the shape that appeared in his headlight beams. But in his peaceful state, neither the dark form nor the impact really registered. Reflexively Lupe put his foot on the brake pedal, but it was far too late. A body flipped over his hood and bounced back toward the curb.

Earlier that evening Sweeps had been arguing that the idea that an event
has a single cause obscures, even denies, the actual nature of causality.
Any single reason, he said, was just one bit of glistening foam riding the
wave of a thousand factors whose vectors converged on a single moment. A minute alteration of any one of them and the event would not
occur.

Had Lupe's transaction taken fifteen seconds longer, had he chosen
not to drive up Clayton, had Bear not fired his final shot, Angelo would
not have been hurt. The other point of view that Sweeps argued, that we
have a predetermined load of karma, construed the same events, but
came to a radically different conclusion.

As Lupe's foot left the brake, a surge of adrenaline overrode his cotton-
soft calm. He jammed his foot down on the accelerator pedal, took the
near corner on two wheels, tore down another block, turned left and left
again, and sped out of the neighborhood. A mile away, he checked his
mirror and stopped beside a warehouse. He checked his mirror again
and got out of the car. He checked the damage. The right front light
housing was dented and the headlight angled its beam crazily across the
road. He wiped the whole area clean with his handkerchief, dropped the
cloth into the gutter and drove home. After he double-locked his front
door and placed the heroin in a hidden safe, he slipped off his clothes,
grasped the warm nude body of his sleeping girlfriend and almost in-
stantly fell asleep.

CHAPTER 31

Call the medic

Feeling helpless, I go out
To meet the moon
Only to find every mountain
Veiled with cloud.

Shigematsu

ASY SAW THE ACCIDENT HAPPEN. As the car roared away, he raced toward the body which sprawled like a rag doll against a telephone pole. Angelo's face was covered with blood; his legs stuck out at impossible angles. When he saw he was in front of the Clayton house, Easy ran up the steps and beat crazily on the glass of the front door. Finding the door unlocked, he pushed it open and yelled, "Hey! Someone get help! A guy's hit down here—bad."

He raced back to the curb, almost colliding with an old man in a faded purple bathrobe and matching slippers padding up to the body. "Stay back. Don't touch him!" Easy said as he tried to remember what medics did. God, he thought, this is when you need heroin! At least, a morphine packet.

He hesitated, took a deep breath and stepped closer. Where he touched the body, blood stuck to his fingers. He rubbed his hand on his pants. He took a handkerchief from his back pocket and wiped the blood out of Angelo's eyes. Gingerly, he pressed his handkerchief down on what seemed to be the source of the bleeding.

Sweeps had heard the shots, but kept reading. Only after Easy's shout did he come down the stairs and step outside. Easy looked up briefly as Sweeps came over to him. "Jesus," Sweeps said. His stomach churned.

"Call a medic, will you?"

"Sure. Sure." Sweeps turned away, frightened and more than a little queasy. Nitrous Eddie and Moonflower were standing just inside the door. "Eddie, call an ambulance," Sweeps said. "Some guy's been hit by a car." Eddie sprinted for the phone.

"Is it bad?" Moonflower asked.

"Looks awful."

They went back into the street. A small crowd stood on the curb. "He's alive," Easy said, glancing over his shoulder. "We've called for help. Don't anybody touch him."

Angelo took his time walking up the hill to the tennis court. He fingered the branches of each blueberry bush along the back of the house, pulling off ripe berries, leaning forward to eat them, sucking them out of his palm, careful not to stain his whites. The summer's blend of rain, sun and humidity had made the bushes heavy with fruit. It was the best crop he'd seen in the six years since his father had insisted the family leave New York City and "homestead in the wilds of Connecticut," as his father called buying a house in the strip of affluent commuter communities that included Stamford.

"Angelo! Come on, boy!" His father's words were not a request but a command. The tone always irritated Angelo.

Wiping his mouth with the back of his hand, he ambled the rest of the way up the lawn to the court. His father, already in position, was nimbly bouncing a ball from one side of his racket to the other.

Angelo twisted the wing nuts on his press until the racket came free. He dropped the press near the door of the court and turned to face his father. "Rally for a few minutes?"

"Sure." His father neatly served a ball near Angelo's feet.

Angelo dropped back gracefully, flipped his hair out of his eyes and sent the ball to his father's backhand. His father ran around it, took on his forehand and slapped the ball into the net. He pulled another ball from his pocket and lobbed it over. Angelo dropped back to get it, but his return fell within easy reach of his father, whose hard forehand return skimmed the top of the net. The ball landed deep in Angelo's far court. Angelo ran for it, but he was too late to even swing.

"Ready?" his father asked after a few more volleys.

"Yo. Want to start serving?"

His father's first serve went long, but the second was good, with a spin on it that foreshortened the bounce, forcing Angelo to move out of position. His father lobbed the return back over Angelo's head, sending him running to the back court. Angelo's return was center court but outside.

"Just out," his father hooted. "Five love. First point to the short-haired father."

"Remember Samson," Angelo called back, running his hand ostentatiously through his dark shoulder-length hair before taking his stance.

At college, Angelo had real coaching for the first time. Now he placed balls carefully, favoring his father every few shots. He chopped the ball and rushed the net more often than he would have against a better player. He tried for spectacular shots, aiming at imaginary handkerchiefs in the far corners when a shot dropped safely in midcourt could have given him the point. In several games, he favored his father's strong forehand and deliberately let a few of his own first serves go long. His father won the first set 6-4.

Angelo took the second 7-5. Between sets his father said, "Wheee, your second serve has improved. Have you grown?"

"About an inch."

His father squinted, measuring Angelo against the wire loops of the back court fence. "You six foot now?"

"Just over."

Angelo had finished his sophomore year ranked seventh on the varsity team, a respectable position in an Ivy League school whose only sports of distinction were swimming, lacrosse and tennis. He was a steady player, more analytical than heroic. He'd studied his father's game and knew his weaknesses.

Into the third set, his father was tiring. Angelo double-faulted a few times to compensate. At 6-6, his father, puffing heavily, stood at the net for a moment after missing a ball down the inside edge of the alley.

"One more game. Let that decide it."

"Sure, Dad. I'm beat."

It was his father's serve. Angelo ran all over the court and, narrowly missing a backhand, gave his father the game and match.

As they walked back toward the house, his father gently grabbed the back of Angelo's neck. "Yale can still win, but it's getting damn hard," he said. Angelo pulled himself free. After his father went inside, Angelo doubled back and ate several handfuls of blueberries.

At dinner—ham slices with raisins set in translucent sauce, corn on the cob, lettuce and tomatoes with French dressing, and lime jello—Angelo and his father argued about national politics. His father called him a naive, pinko liberal; Angelo in turn branded his father a reactionary Republican Neanderthal. Neither acknowledged the sharp edge in their joking. Angelo's mother, as usual, added little to the discussion. After dinner Angelo declined their invitation to watch television and went up to his room.

Sprawled on his bed, he plunged back into *one hundred dollar misunderstanding*, which Dan had pressed on him. "One-handed reading," Dan said. "Ideal for your level of development." As Angelo read, he grinned often, even laughed aloud a few times. He felt superior to the priggish, white college-boy hero, and certainly to the street-smart fourteen-year-old black prostitute. One of her monologues gave him an erection; that pleased him even more. He hadn't been turned on by a book since *Candy*.

Later, there was a knock on his bedroom door.

"Come in," Angelo said.

"Just wanted to say goodnight. I enjoyed our game."

"Thanks, Dad. So did I."

"You know in the third set you double-faulted a few times."

"Nobody's perfect. Even Gonzales doubles sometimes."

"I watched you play against Columbia."

"I remember."

"Angelo, when you give the other guy an advantage he doesn't deserve, he feels patronized. When you play, play your best."

Angelo started to speak. His father reached over and gripped his shoulder. "I still liked winning." He left the room.

Angelo wondered if his father really saw through his whole strategy but was playing a still deeper game, mentioning only the most obvious maneuvers, like giving up a few pawns to retain control of the rest of the board.

The next day Angelo took the first set 6-3. "My God," his father said, lying on the grass and wiping his face with his handkerchief. "I still think it's crazy for you to take this job in lieu of a junior semester abroad."

"If I tripped off to Europe taking Mickey Mouse classes in Paris like you did, you'd think that was cool."

"That was different. I was learning a language."

"And getting laid, I'll bet."

"Watch your mouth, young man."

"Aw, get off it, Dad."

"What language can you learn in San Francisco? Chinese?"

"You wouldn't care as long as I didn't marry one."

"Have I ever said a word about whom you should marry?"

"No, sorry. That's Mom's responsibility." Pressing one hand over his chest, he wrapped the other over it and imitated his mother's habitual look of constricted concern. In a higher pitched voice, he said, "You can marry anyone you wish, of course. But it's soooo much easier if she understands our world."

His father's face showed no amusement. "Your mother's right, you know."

"I know, I know. Anyone in the world—as long as she's welcome at the country club."

"Not so stupid to think about who your friends will be."

"Unless—may Heaven smite me—I am not interested in making scads of money and joining a country club." Angelo stood up and began to walk back toward the court.

His father sat up. "Easy enough for you to say." He paused for effect. "With a father who pays your school bills."

"Don't take it out on me. Is it my fault I was born to parents who can afford them?"

"Well, you could cut your hair."

Angelo looked away from his father, through the fence, down into the courtyard where the cobblestones were still shiny from last night's thunderstorm. The middle garage door was open, a dark arched hole flanked by two oak pillars. He twirled the racket between his hands. "Let it grow long is what I was told. Just doing what my employer ordered. That kind of subservience should make you proud."

They resumed their game. His father's first serve went long. His second serve was a soft lob that landed just over the net. Angelo raced for it and missed.

Angelo returned his father's next serve from midcourt. They played the ball back and forth a few times before Angelo placed it just out of reach of his father's backhand.

Coming to the net to pick up a ball, his father said, "Hope you keep up your tennis. Will you have time?"

"Don't know. I'm just a peon on the project."

"Well, don't get involved with a native is all that I ask. No strange girls who smoke marijuana and would love to come to Connecticut."

"How about a leggy blonde tennis player with a degree from Stanford whose father owns a bank?"

"Very astringent humor."

"I've an astringent father."

Angelo lost the next few points and the game. Taking the serve, he delivered three aces in a row. He won the game with a slam from the net that his father didn't even try to stop. "Anywhere in Stamford or Greenwich where I can get some West Coast hip clothes, maybe some deerskin moccasins?" he asked. He flipped a ball to his father. He anticipated and thus doubly enjoyed his father's pained expression.

"We haven't had Indian clothes around here since we ran them out of their wigwams. If you need clothes, go to J. Press," he snapped.

Angelo returned a ball down the middle, then hit the return out of bounds. What was the point? He was leaving soon enough. "Thanks for the offer. I will." He flicked the hair off his forehead. His father's eyes followed the movement as his shaggy hair fell back over his neck.

"At least you can go out there looking decent." His father's voice was strident.

Angelo strolled to the net, popped a ball onto his racket and bounced it into his hand. "My father used to tell me, 'It's what's inside that counts.'"

"My son used to like looking good."

"Maybe it's a phase I'm going through."

"Hope so."

A wave of pain passed through Angelo, erasing his father's face and the fence behind him. He opened his eyes and didn't know what he was seeing. It was dark and someone was touching him. He couldn't move his legs. He passed out from the pain.

CHAPTER 32

Finnbar steps out

There is nothing I can give you
which you have not;
but there is much, very much,
that, while I can not give it, you can take.

Fra Giovanni

ARLIER THAT EVENING, Finnbar had told the monsignor he'd
be visiting a sick parishioner and not to wait up. The older
man, while pleased that Father O'Malley was actually doing
meaningful work, had no intention of staying up in any case.

Moonflower met Finnbar outside the Print Mint and gave him a full
body hug. "You didn't cop out on me," she said as she pressed her pelvis
against his. "You feel terrific."

Terrified that someone would recognize him, he turned down her
idea of coffee at the Blue Unicorn.

"We can go back to my place," she said. She noted his hesitation,
thinking he was surely the most timid guy who'd ever turned her on.
"It's cool. Not really my place. A bunch of us."

The coffee made him edgy. He followed it with a glass of milk that he hoped would relax his nervous stomach.

Later, in her room, after many attempts and endless hesitations, he managed to tell her that he was a priest. She hooted with laughter. "Hey, Finnbar, you are terrific. Far out! A holy in-the-hay roller, is that it?"

"Really! I'm an ordained priest."

"So what kind is that?"

"I'm a Catholic."

"No! You look so healthy."

"This isn't funny to me."

Moonflower rolled onto her stomach. "Well, if we're into heavy truth telling, I'm Jewish. So we're almost even. Except in my parents' house getting it on with you is worse for me than getting it on with me in your parents' house could ever be."

"I don't follow that," he said.

"In your house you all trade prayers for forgiveness. Couple dozen Hail Marys and your windshield's wiped clean. In my house—no deals—no forgiveness—no way."

They lay apart in the darkness, each reconsidering the situation.

Moonflower almost laughed. Who'd have thought it! A used-to-be-nice Jewish girl half undressed, lying on a mattress, without a box spring even. Next to her, with a hard-on as big as a ballpark Polish, a real cross-and-candles priest.

"No forgiveness?" he repeated.

"One day a year, on Yom Kippur, we get the command. Forgive everybody. The service goes on all day. No one in my family ever sat it through or forgave anybody, far as I know."

"Don't you believe that God forgives you?"

"Next time he drops by, I'll ask him. My father, who art in Brookline, won't." She envisioned her father hopping about the kitchen, acting out the soap opera, pulling on his own hair and shouting, "My daughter mit a priest? I have no daughter! Oy! Oy!" She knew her father was not emotional enough, Jewish enough or even concerned enough to do anything of the kind. He'd probably say to Mom, "Your crazy daughter! At least she's not doing it in the neighborhood."

"Shall I leave?" Finnbar asked in a very unsure voice.

"Hell, no!" she said. "I didn't get us up here to have you turn tail. Finnbar, you are a most cool and special dude. And if you're a little weirder than I thought—and you are—pile it on me, baby." She rolled over on him.

Later on, Finnbar having been relieved of most of his clothes, along with, layer by layer, his hesitations, his moral concerns but not his shyness, they clung to each other like two magnets.

He had thought Moonflower brazen and aggressively sexual. He was amazed to find that she was deeply afraid of not being wanted and needed desperately to be seen as a person in her own right. "I want to be a singer, to move people, to have them crave me, scream for me. I don't care about money. I want adoration. No critics, just fans."

Finnbar kissed Moonflower's cheek, then her neck. She cooed with pleasure. Finnbar pushed hesitantly at her ear with his nose, wishing he could say to her that he'd never done this before.

"Wow, an ordained priest," she said, giggling. "Yes, Toto, I know we're not in Boston anymore."

Able, in brief bursts, to meet her openness with his own, he told her how frightened he was of everything out here, how excited he'd been at the Be-In and how guilty he'd felt afterward. "I really wanted to touch you—your breasts."

"What a relief. I thought maybe you were a fairy or something."

"I hadn't an inkling it would be all right with you."

"Lost moments of bliss," she said.

He didn't tell her of the nights since the Be-In when he'd awakened with an erection. How he'd sit up and pray until it went away. Just two nights ago he'd dreamed that Evelyn, who'd treated him as a nobody in high school, was touching his penis.

He pulled away from Moonflower. "This is not a good idea."

"Finn," she said, skating her fingers along his thigh. "Let me worry about our bodies. You worry about our souls."

"I am."

"I know." She ran her other hand down his chest, stopping just below his navel. "Stop worrying or else."

He sighed. "I've stopped."

"I love it when you lie." Her hand started down again.

"I'm worrying. I'm worrying."

"Now I believe you," she said.

He had kept his jockey shorts on, his erection pulsing uncomfortably against the fabric. Moonflower, at his insistence, still wore her panties.

At that moment, Angelo had opened the desk drawer. When he bolted into the street with Bear behind him, Moonflower and Finnbar began to kiss. As Angelo raced around the corner onto Clayton, Moonflower was licking Finnbar's back teeth. When the last shot was fired, she was slipping her hand into Finnbar's shorts.

"What was that?" Finnbar's head jerked up.

"My hand, obviously."

His shorts were half off when Lupe's car drifted around the corner.

At the sound of Easy's shout, Finnbar rolled away from Moonflower. She put on a slip and ran out. He scrabbled around on the floor for his undershirt, afraid he'd be seen, afraid she'd come back, afraid she wouldn't. He dressed in the dark, went down the back stairs and out the door. He boosted himself over the fence and ran across a small backyard. A dog barked, but Finnbar was gone before it got to the window to snarl at the blackness. He let himself out a gate and raced away, unnoticed.

Sweeps pushed through the people until he was beside Easy. "Eddie
called an ambulance. Anything else we can do?"

"Shit. I don't know. Get some towels maybe," Easy said.

Moonflower hurried back out with two towels. Easy used one to
prop up Angelo's bleeding head and the other to wipe away more blood.
Moonflower looked closely, then screamed. "Oh God—it's Angelo!"

She charged up the stairs and burst into Shadow's room. "Honey, it's
Angelo. He's been hit by a car!" Shadow grunted and rolled over. Moonflower shook her into wakefulness. Naked and groggy, she finally
grabbed a big sweater, pulled it over her head and headed for the stairs,
shaking her hair out of her eyes. As she came out the front door a police
siren sounded.

At first all she could see was the crowd, but as they drew back for the
police, she could make out Angelo lying on the curb. Two officers were
slowly lifting one leg up and moving it toward the other.

Moonflower patted her shoulder. "They're being real careful."

Shadow started forward, but Moonflower stopped her. "Let them do
their job."

The officers had cut the cloth away from Angelo's legs by the time
the ambulance arrived. The paramedics took over, immobilizing his legs
and head. But when they slipped a stretcher under him, a low moan
came from his throat like the whine of a dog. They carried him into the
ambulance and closed the doors.

Shadow ran around to the driver's window and tapped on it. The
glass rolled down a few inches. "Where are you taking him?"

"UC Emergency Room. Right up the hill." The driver looked down
at Shadow's legs, and she realized she was naked except for the sweater.
She hunched down as he rolled up his window. The ambulance pulled
away, its flashing red lights bouncing off walls and windows along the
street. When it backed up, one rear tire rolled over the vials of LSD,
smashing the few not already broken into fragments.

Awakened by the first shot, Brad ran downstairs just after Bear opened the front door. His bare toe touched the bullet hole in the hardwood floor. He turned on the lights and saw the open desk drawer and the half-empty drug box. When Bear returned, full of himself and his "going after the son of a bitch who'd tried for seconds," Brad said nothing.

"I think I nicked the bastard," Bear chortled. "At least I scared the shit out of him." He went up the stairs, fondling the gun. At the top he turned and sighted along the barrel at Brad. "If it hadn't been so dark, I could have gotten him from here." Bear went into his room and locked the door.

Brad shivered in the open hallway. Back in his own room, he noted Angelo's unmade bed, assumed that he was with Shadow and went to sleep.

By the time Shadow and Sweeps arrived at the emergency room, Angelo was already in surgery. The night nurse at the counter looked over his chart. Both legs broken. Multiple fractures. Skull fractures likely. Probable internal injuries, severe blood loss. "He's banged up in a lot of places," she said. "They've given him two quarts of Ringer's already. It boosts blood volume. The lab's got a rush order to get his blood typed so they can start transfusions." She hung up the chart and looked past them to the next person.

They didn't move. She looked at them again. "He's hurt pretty badly, but we're as good as he can get."

Shadow bit her lip. "Can I see him?"

"Call tomorrow. Normal visiting hours are from one to three-thirty." She glanced back at his chart. "Are you family?"

They looked at each other. "Not exactly," Sweeps said.

"If you can get hold of a relative, it would help."

Shadow had already turned away. Sweeps followed her out of the building. They walked home in silence. As they turned onto Clayton, Sweeps asked, "Where's he from?"

"Connecticut. He didn't tell me much about himself. I know where he works."

"Good. We'll try there." Sweeps put his hand on the back of her neck. "We can't do a thing till tomorrow."

"Oh, Sweeps!" Shadow grabbed him tight around the waist and pressed herself into his chest. "Thanks."

He kissed the top of her head. "Go to bed. Try to sleep." Ashamed of his momentary sexual rush, he pulled away. "Easy's who you should thank."

"You, too," she said.

In his room, Finnbar replayed and repented the evening. He stared at a small Christ carved from black wood hanging on a cross on the wall. He worried his rosary like a dog shaking a dry bone.

The doctors cleaned and bandaged Angelo's skull, and set and cast each leg. Lactated Ringer's solution dripped into his arm until it was replaced with a bottle containing whole blood. He remained in the intensive care unit all night. By morning, he still had not regained consciousness and his vital signs remained low. As his condition was stable, however, he was moved to a private room and monitored.

CHAPTER 33

Looking after Angelo

*From one point of view
creatures are simply tubes,
putting things in one end
and pushing them out the other
—until the tubes wear out.*

Alan Watts

SWEEPS WONDERED when he saw that Angelo's place adjoined the whorehouse, but he didn't say anything. "I'll go in," he told Shadow. She waited for him on the sidewalk.

"Wouldn't believe me until they'd checked the hospital," he reported when he came out. "They're calling his parents. Creepy bunch."

Back at the house, they each ate an apple and some slices off a brick of jack cheese. Shadow poured herself a glass of milk and one for Sweeps. They divided the few remaining Oreos.

Alone in her room, Shadow cried onto the belly of her stuffed bear until she feel asleep. Sweeps was in the living room talking to Easy when she came downstairs to go to the hospital.

The three of them walked slowly up the steep hill to the main entrance.

"Angelo Borden?" said the man at the front desk. "He's in 403." He looked them over. "Relatives only."

"We're his family," Easy said, and strode past the clerk to the elevators. Shadow and Sweeps ran after him. When one elevator opened they saw that it was huge, with doors on both ends, walls and floor of shiny steel, the ceiling a featureless gunmetal gray. It depressed and intimidated them. At the fourth floor they walked onto a dimly lit ward with a nursing station that stood like a sentry box in the center of the hallway. The duty nurse stared at them through half-glasses. Sweeps hastily tucked in his shirt and pushed his hair back behind his ears. Easy inched himself up to military erectness.

"We'd like to see Angelo Borden," Shadow said as politely as she could. The nurse was silent. "He was brought in last night, late."

The nurse turned and consulted the clipboards hanging on the wall behind her. "I'm afraid you can't. He's not conscious." She turned back to them. "Are you relatives?"

Tears filled Shadow's eyes. She looked down at the floor and, sobbing quietly, shook her head.

After a long silence, the nurse sighed and dropped her shoulders a fraction. "But you can't stay." She pushed open the waist-high door. "Come with me."

They clung together, following her down the corridor, separating only to avoid empty gurneys and racks crowded with bottles, tubes and straps. The nurse pushed open a door. Easy hung back while the others went in.

In the artificial half-light of a windowless room, Angelo lay with an IV tube strapped to one arm, wires disappearing into his chest. Lights blinked on and off on a machine humming softly at the foot of his bed. Only Angelo's ears, eyes, nostrils, mouth and chin were visible under the bandages. The wire frame that held the covers off his legs made it look as if he had been pushed halfway into a cloth-covered packing box.

"Angelo?" Shadow said. "It's me, Shadow."

"He can't hear you," the nurse said. She tapped the chart she'd pulled off a metal holder. "Multiple skull fractures." She looked over her glasses as if seeing Sweeps and Shadow for the first time. "What happened?"

"He was crossing the street," Sweeps said.

"Poor kid." The nurse frowned as she read the chart. "He's had a rough night. Casts on both legs. Multiple transfusions. They operated on him twice. Took some chips of bone out of his head this morning."

Shadow began to shake. She leaned back onto Sweeps. "Could we stay? We'll be real quiet."

The nurse stiffened. "I'm sorry. I shouldn't have even let you in."

Outside Easy watched two orderlies in green smocks roll an empty gurney into the elevator. A janitor limped by, carrying a large oval pail with a mop-squeezer welded to its edge. Easy noticed the neat stacks of sheets, pillowcases, towels, toilet paper, Kleenex boxes, plastic bowls, flower vases and dressing gowns on the shelves of a supply closet. Mattress pads and green gowns were piled on a bottom shelf. Nurses passed him carrying coffee cups. Easy could hear them chattering at the end of the hall. He pressed his back against the wall, uncomfortably recalling the mental ward of the Palo Alto Veterans Hospital.

In the elevator, Shadow wept. "He's so alone there."

"Want to come back tonight?" Easy asked.

"Not likely. It's all rules and witch-bitch nurses," Sweeps said.

Easy smiled. When they reached the street doors, he hung back. "Wait for me outside," he said, and went back in. Sweeps and Shadow stood together on the steps. The sunlight barely pierced the cloud cover, casting a pale, shadowless light. Soon Easy reappeared with a cloth bundle. He sailed past them down the steps.

"What's that?" Shadow asked when they caught up with him.

"You'll see," Easy said, without breaking stride. He stopped after rounding the corner. Hopping up and down with pleasure, he displayed two green gowns and two caps. "Piece of cake. Hospitals build everything alike. I went to the third floor supply closet like I was supposed to be there. Stayed cool. Picked up the stuff, waltzed out. Nobody even looked up."

Shadow looked from Easy to the uniforms and back to Easy. She shook her head. "I don't get it."

"Tonight, Sweeps and I walk right in. On the night shift nobody does shit for the patients. Believe me, I know. We're in. We visit."

"What about me?" Shadow asked.

Easy refolded the gowns and wrapped them in his jacket. "I got another idea for you."

When Bear and Brad arrived on the fourth floor, they too were told that the patient was unconscious and could not be visited. Bear, who'd put on a tie and was wearing his jacket, put his hands on the small counter. His fingertips flattened as he pressed on the plastic covering. He pushed his face into the opening. "Listen. I'm his uncle. My sister's flying out tonight. You let me in." The nurse blanched and started to reply, then thought better of it. She let them into the room.

Bear pulled up the bottom of the sheet and examined the casts. He leaned down and looked into Angelo's pale yellow face. "Jesus H. Christ," he muttered. Brad stayed at the foot of the bed, numb and silent.

Back on the street, Bear slammed a fist into his open hand. "This goddamned project is jinxed. Ripped off. Everything fucking crazy with Langwater. Ripped off again, and now this!"

"Is he going to be all right?"

"How the hell should I know?" Bear shrugged. "He'll pull through. Don't you start in whining. I need someone around who's not trouble."

At three that morning, Easy woke Shadow and Sweeps. He woke Moon-flower too, but she told him where to put his good deeding and went back to sleep. As the three trudged up the hill, Easy and Sweeps poked each other and joked about Moonflower. Just short of the main entrance, Easy stopped. "Let's walk around."

The nearest side door was lit by a single bulb in a yellow glass cover dimmed by layers of dirt. Easy tried the door but it was locked. "Perfect," he said. "Wait here."

He rolled up his sleeves and put on one of the green outfits. Shoving his hair under the cap, he made a victory sign and headed back toward the main entrance. Inside, the guard at the front desk glanced up. "Locked myself out having a smoke," Easy said. The guard grunted and returned to his newspaper.

Down the hall a door capped by a green exit sign opened onto a cement stairwell. Easy gently pushed it open. Sweeps was already dressed in the other gown and cap. Gesturing to them to make no noise, Easy led the other two up one flight.

Easy pressed Shadow's arm. "Stay put till we come get you. You dig?" He pushed the inner door open a crack. Then he gestured to Sweeps. The two sauntered down the hall and stopped at the first empty gurney.

Easy walked into a supply closet and came back with two sheets that he pitched onto the gurney. They rolled it toward the exit door. Easy opened the inside door and beckoned to Shadow. When she came in, Easy pointed to the gurney. She hopped on and lay down. Easy pulled a sheet over her up to her nose and pushed the gurney to the elevator. When it opened, he motioned Sweeps in and pushed the gurney in after him. The doors closed. Sweeps and Shadow snorted with laughter. "Shhh," Easy said. "We're doing good, aren't we?"

"One more river to cross," Sweeps said.

The elevator doors opened. The two men rolled the gurney deliberately past the nursing station. Two nurses playing cards barely gave them a glance. The hallway outside Angelo's room was empty and dark except at the far end, where light from the street cast a pale square onto the scuffed green and black linoleum triangles.

Shadow rolled off the gurney and slipped into the room. Sweeps followed, holding the door for Easy who shook his head. "Come on!" Sweeps whispered.

"I don't like it in there," Easy said. "I'll stand watch. If anyone comes, I'll tap the door with my foot. You duck into the bathroom."

"It's your deal," Sweeps said, and eased the door closed. Easy positioned the gurney across the doorway, and stood against the wall.

Shadow fumbled around in the dark until she found the small table lamp. Angelo's breathing was slow and regular. There was no expression on his face, not even the slackness of sleep. Fluid dripped from a bottle into his arm. The little machine hummed, its lights flickering steadily.

There was a light kick on the door. "Yes, ma'am," they heard Easy say. Shadow and Sweeps leapt into the tiny bathroom. Shadow stepped on the toilet seat and Sweeps stood in front of it. She wrapped her arms around his forehead.

A nurse entered, wheeling a rack. She checked Angelo's pulse, listened to his breathing and made notations on his chart. She stood for a moment looking into his immobile face and replaced the almost empty IV bottle. She crossed herself, then turned and left.

Easy came in and tapped on the bathroom door. "All clear," he whispered, and let himself back out into the hall.

Shadow moved to the edge of the bed. She stroked Angelo's face. When she kissed his lips, his breathing stopped for a few seconds, then resumed again. She licked his ear. Again his breathing faltered. She held his hand, slack as a beanbag, and laid it against her face.

"Go out for a while," she whispered.

Without a word Sweeps left. Easy took advantage of having company to go to the toilet. When he returned, the two stood together in silence.

Shadow kissed Angelo's ear again, pushing her tongue deep into it. His breathing became irregular, then flattened out. She kicked off her shoes and pulled her sweater over her head.

Ten minutes later, she emerged from the room, her face flushed. "I think he'll be better tomorrow," she whispered, running her hands through her hair. She hauled herself onto the gurney and pulled the sheet up.

CHAPTER 34

Each one a specialist

The butterfly
Resting on the temple bell
Asleep.

Buson

THE NEXT AFTERNOON, Shadow, dressed in a blue skirt and a blue-green sweater, her hair tied back in a ponytail, presented herself at the downstairs desk. She asked about Angelo. The man on duty said, "The family just went up."

She took the elevator to the third floor and climbed the stairs to the fourth. She walked to the lounge near the nursing station and pretended to read a magazine. At the other end of the room, a man and woman stood close together. Although their hands were touching, each looked off in a different direction.

A heavyset doctor came over to them. "Mr. and Mrs. Borden? I'm Doctor Abrams." He paused and looked between them. "We're continuing transfusions, but there is still considerable internal bleeding. We're hoping his system will stabilize."

"Should he be moved somewhere else?" Mr. Borden asked. "Some kind of specialist?" His voice broke.

"Mr. Borden," the doctor spread his hands, "there are four of us already, each one a specialist." He folded his arms across his chest and looked out the window. "Frankly, what we need is a miracle, or at least some exceptionally good luck."

Mr. Borden groped for his wife's hand.

"Is it all those fractures?" she asked.

"I'm sorry, Mrs. Borden, it's not just that. He lost a lot of blood. His heart muscles aren't contracting vigorously enough. For a little while last night, his chart recorded a normal period. That was a very positive sign."

Angelo's father sagged into a chair. "There must be something you can do," he said.

"We just have to wait." The doctor touched his arm and walked away.

Mrs. Borden turned to her husband; her thin face was tight and gray. Under her eyes, dark circles were visible through her makeup. "I'm going to sit with him and pray."

Left alone, sunk in a chair, Mr. Borden rubbed the backs of his knees against the frayed cushion. After a few minutes, he stood and headed after his wife.

Shadow went up to the nurses' station. "Excuse me. Is Angelo Borden any better?"

"Is he a good friend of yours?" Their eyes met for a moment. The nurse, her hair hanging in two pigtails, seemed only a little older than Shadow. Her cheeks were a smooth, bright rose, as if they were scrubbed too often. "His parents are in there now."

"I know."

The nurse continued to meet Shadow's gaze. "Oh, it's like that?"

Shadow bit her lip and nodded.

"Do they know about you?"

Shadow shook her head.

The nurse's pigtails swung back and forth. "The doctors weren't sure he'd last the night." Shadow made a little bleat.

"But he did." The nurse turned and looked at a sheet on her desk, clicking a pencil against her teeth. "D. I. C."

"What's that?"

"Disseminated intervascular coagulopathy. It happens after major trauma sometimes, especially if there are a lot of transfusions." The nurse looked past Shadow. "He's seeping blood. Like he's weeping internally."

Shadow shuddered. "What do they do for it?"

"They wait." The nurse reached out and touched Shadow's hand. "And they hope."

Shadow looked down the hall.

"Visiting hours end at three-thirty. But I'm on till five. If you come in after they go"—she flipped one thumb down the hall—"I'll let you in."

"You're so nice."

"I know how it is." Her cheeks turned a deeper shade of rose. "I'm with a guy and my parents don't know. They'd kill me."

Shadow walked down to the park. She stood for a long time at the bottom of a hill planted with rhododendrons. A few had new leaves, but it was too early in the year for anything more than the first buds. When she went home, she told Sweeps what the nurse had said.

He put his fingers together and blew into them. He was silent for a long time. "I'm going back tonight. Want to come?"

CHAPTER 35

Angelo
and the Bardo Thödol

Difficulty at the beginning works supreme success,
furthering through perseverance.
It furthers one to appoint helpers.

I Ching, Hexagram 3, "Chun"

WHEN SWEEPS TAPPED ON HER DOOR, Shadow sat up, startled. She'd fallen asleep still dressed. They entered the hospital as they had before. After the night nurse made her check, Sweeps opened the sack he carried. He set up two candles, one on each of the square white tables near the head of the bed, and lit them. Then he sat close to Angelo's head and took out a book.

"What's that?"

"An instruction book—from Tibet."

"From where?"

"It's to help him make the transition. If he's going." Sweeps sat with his eyes closed, the book in his lap for several minutes. Then he leaned close and, glancing at the book, whispered into Angelo's ear. Shadow rocked her chair.

"What are you saying?" she said after a while.

Sweeps held up a hand and continued as before. After a few more minutes of whispering, he relaxed against the back of his chair.

"Say it out loud," Shadow hissed.

"Okay, but the first time had to be private."

He opened the book and, moving his finger across the lines, began to intone the words, his voice rising and falling as if he was singing medieval plainsong.

Oh nobly born Angelo,
Beloved of us here.
Your time has come
To seek reality.
Your breathing may soon cease.
Set free, you will see the Pure Light.
Set free, you will see the Bardo.
The state where all things are as void as a cloudless sky.
Pay attention to these words:
Do not allow yourself to be distracted
By other thoughts or memories.
Remain lucid and calm.
Bear in mind what you hear.
If you suffer, do not give way to the pain.
If restful numbness overtakes you, do not surrender.
If peaceful forgetting fills you, do not give in.
Remain watchful and alert!
Remain watchful and alert!
Remain watchful and alert!

Shadow pulled a Kleenex from the box on the bedside table and wiped her nose and eyes.

Nobly born Angelo,

Your mind now separates from your body.
Rouse your energy,
So that you enter this state self-possessed
And in full consciousness.

Sweeps began again.

Shadow rocked on her chair and stared at one of the candles. She remembered when her family had gone to Greek Orthodox Easter service with her parents' friends, the Votakos. The church was dark except for one candle. As she sat on her mother's lap, the chanting almost put her to sleep. Then it became louder and more animated. Her mother let her stand on her lap to see. The priest passed the lighted candle to a choirboy. He turned around and lit three candles held by others, who turned to those behind them, each lighting three more. A slow wave of flickering lights flowed back, row after row, until every face in the church was illuminated by the light of a candle.

"Remain watchful and alert!" Sweeps repeated. Shadow went to the other side of the bed and knelt beside Angelo and held his hand. On the third repetition, Sweeps sang the words, his voice growing softer and softer until, at the end, he leaned over and whispered, "In full consciousness."

The machine at the foot of the bed ceased its hum.

"Oh, nobly born Angelo," Sweeps chanted, his lips almost touching Angelo's ear.

Now you are experiencing the light of Pure Reality,
Not formed into any separate thing.
Do not worry.
Do not withdraw.
A dull smoky light shines beside the Pure Light.
Do not look toward it.
It feeds on fear.
It is created from anger.

Put your faith in the light.
Go toward the light.
Take refuge in the light.

Shadow watched his finger hesitate, then continue across the page.

Whatever you see are only illusions.
Demons, the angels, even the gods.
All illusions.
Turn back to the light.
Remember the light.
You do this for the happiness and liberation of all beings.

Shadow wept. She stood and went to stand behind Sweeps, her hands resting on his shoulders. The yellow tint began to recede from Angelo's face.

Do not forget these words!
Remain vigilant and alert!
Remain calm and alert.

Shadow pushed the empty chair into a corner. Shaking off her sandals, she dropped her skirt to the floor. In the flickering candlelight, her body barely visible against the dark walls, her belly smooth and flat, her hips narrowed by a skintight black leotard, she danced. Her shadow flowed over the bed and slid along the wall.

Her feet made soft slaps on the floor as she arched from side to side. She moved in slow undulations. She moved close to the bed and then, in a series of such tiny steps that dozens of movements carried her no more than a foot away, she danced Angelo's shyness. She danced his leaning into a room until he felt welcome. She danced his initial fears, his confusion in their coming together. She danced their walking to the Be-In, and his walk back home. She danced Angelo's journey into himself, and into the ten thousand worlds beyond.

Sweeps began to chant again, matching his words to her movements. She danced to the words, transforming each through her body. She danced Angelo's soul going toward the light.

She stopped and stood, her feet flat on the floor, one arm extended, the other bent. She recalled his search for understanding and acceptance. Her body exploded in a series of leaps, re-creating his discovery that he was part of the Divine. She danced his joyful thankfulness, pounding the floor with her feet as if it were soft, moist earth.

She started to dance his dying, but stopped. Breathing hard and shaking, she danced her sorrow, danced herself begging him not to die. Sweeps stopped chanting.

Shadow froze. "I'm not finished. Say it again."

Sweeps opened the book. "Oh, nobly born Angelo, beloved of those here with you. . ."

Shadow danced Angelo's dying. In her dance, his heart beat more slowly, his breath stopped, his body stiffened and cooled like spilled wax. She danced his first awareness of his death, the confusion and the terror. She danced the separation of his soul from his body—the surprise and the wonder, then the lightness and ease of it. She danced without knowing what she danced but knowing he would understand it.

Finally she danced his liberation, entering into the Light.

Sweeps fell silent and watched her.

Tears streamed down her face and mixed with sweat, dropped onto the floor. Sweat soaked her leotard. She seemed to be lit from within. She stood at the edge of the bed and brushed Angelo's face with her wet, gleaming hair. Back and forth, her hair stroked his face. The water from her body glistened like diamond dust on his cheeks, which were the color of old piano keys.

She stood up.

"He's gone," she said.

Sweeps nodded and wiped the tears from his cheeks. He blew the candles out and put them back in his sack. He kissed the book as if it were a missal before it too went into the bag. Shadow pulled on her skirt and retrieved her shoes from under the bed. Sweeps took off the green gown. They walked out together.

"The patient in room 403 has left his body," Sweeps said to the startled nurse. She whirled and saw that a monitoring light had turned red. When she turned back, Shadow and Sweeps were gone.

They walked down the stairs and emerged into a night swept clear of fog. The glow from the city lights was so strong that only a few bright stars were visible. Sweeps took off his jacket and put it around Shadow. It covered her almost to her knees, made her look like a child.

Did it do any good to chant the words of the Bardo? He'd find out when he died, maybe. Right then, he'd know, and he'd also know that it didn't matter. The candles bumped against one another as he shifted the sack from one hand to the other.

PART V

CHAPTER 36

Sweeps sweeps

I hear and behold God in every object,
yet understand God not in the least.

Walt Whitman

TWO WEEKS LATER Sweeps was at the kitchen table rereading a postcard that had arrived the day before. It showed a fishing boat in a small harbor. On the back it said, "Oysters aren't as good, but I've got steady work. Destroy this after reading. Frank." The stamp was from Jamaica. Sweeps stuck it on the window ledge over the sink and returned to his breakfast.

"Can I come along to the ballroom?" Shadow's voice was high-pitched and bouncy.

He looked at her, not sure what in her tone made him uneasy.

"I'd like to," she said, and danced across the kitchen to the counter. Without her usual grace, she slathered two slices of bread with peanut butter and grape jelly. She licked the knife clean and, her tongue still on the knife, looked over at Sweeps. She was acting like, even looked like, a twelve-year-old. "Afterwards, you and I can groove to the park, have a picnic or somethin'. Please."

"Sure, kiddo. You can help polish the floor, if you promise to do a good job."

"I will, Sweeps—I really will."

Shadow grabbed hold of one of the dust mops and ran to the front of the ballroom. Prancing back and forth like Charlie Chaplin, she pushed it crazily in every direction. While Sweeps worked, she raced back, clearing a shining track through the dust. She flipped the handle toward him and, before it reached his hands, turned and was gone. She romped up and down the pavilion, circling him from time to time like an excited pony. Whenever Sweeps came near, she bowed, then in great gliding turns, moved down the floor, spun on her heel in midstride and bounded in the opposite direction. She whirled, spreading her arms like hawk wings; rising on her toes, she quivered and began a graceful descent until her hands almost touched the floor.

Eventually she glided back to Sweeps in long steps as if she were ice-skating. She collapsed into a chair, her legs straight and spread, her toes pointing up. "Boy, that was good," she said, wiping her mouth carelessly. She slid onto her knees and clasped her arms around Sweeps' legs. "Take me to the park?" She looked up.

"I'm about done," he said, gently disengaging himself. "Then we'll go. But first back home to stash this stuff."

"You're being very sweet to me." She put one hand on his back. "I know I'm a pest, but I won't be much longer."

He smiled at her. "You're the nicest pest I've ever known."

"Bet you say that to all the pests."

He handed her the mop and push broom. She hugged the poles to her body, then put them over her shoulder as if she intended to march with them. Sweeps picked up the buckets.

On the street, a young man, leaning far out of his second-floor window, called down. "Hey, pretty witch person, can I have a ride on your broom? I'm tired, and I don't know where I'm going to."

"Broom's broken," she shouted, flashing him a smile. "Fell apart last trip to the moon."

"Sorry about that. I just wanted you to know I love you."

Shadow's eyes filled with tears.

"You got a name?" he called.

"Not today," she said, without looking up.

"My name is Truth." He pulled his hair back with one hand and leaned out a few more inches. "Honest," he said in a stage whisper.

Shadow sniffled loudly. "I'm going to the park with my friend."

"Can I come?"

"This is not your day."

"Later, broomgirl," he said, and waved good-bye.

"Do you know him?" Shadow and Sweeps asked one another simultaneously. They laughed and bowed to each other.

It had rained the night before. Sweeps and Shadow sat on a bench and watched battalions of tiny ant-like creatures emerging from cracks in the asphalt. They trailed slicked-down long translucent wings as they surged to the surface, antennas waving in every direction. Once out, their wings snapped open. Then each one took about ten steps, flexed its wings, and became airborne. They fluttered up, rising eight or ten feet and circling each other.

Shadow, mesmerized, took Sweeps' hand.

As if the night's rain had been a signal, hole after hole disgorged insects. Paratroopers in reverse, they moved along their subterranean jump lines to the departure point. As each one inched away, another shiny black head filled the emptied space. By the hundreds, they emerged from the darkness, rose, glided down and rose again. Wind blew most of them into nearby flowerbeds. A few, their tattered wings dragging behind them, crawled into the grass on either side of the path.

Shadow rested her head on Sweeps' shoulder. "Think ants believe in resurrection?" Her eyes again filled with tears. Sweeps squeezed her fingers but said nothing.

Back home, sitting cross-legged on his mattress, Sweeps looked at the books on his bottom shelf. *Independent People, The Peasants, Growth of the Soil.* He'd lent out his Tolstoy. In this neighborhood of dropped-out dopers, flaming radicals, pseudo-Buddhists and loopy, directionless kids, people were always borrowing books. How different, he mused. At Stanford, rarely did anyone even notice what I was reading.

Running his fingers over the spines of the books, he wondered if he'd ever go back. He still kept a couple of boxes of his class notes just in case. According to the university, he hadn't dropped out. His file probably was labeled:

`Indefinite leave of absence.`

`Pursuing alternate short-range career goals.`

Goosed along by two "we love education" parents and a system that elevated those who avoided making their own decisions, he'd found that comparative literature was the easiest path. That he wouldn't be drafted if he was in graduate school was the final deciding factor.

He sniffed the books. A faint smell of Cubberley Library clung to them. He recalled the first time he'd gone to the library stoned. In his carrel he'd spread out his notes, opened and closed a couple of books, then shuffled his notes into small piles. He'd put his chin on his hands and stared at the line of books on the small, lacquered maple shelf. Novels supported slim journals of literary criticism. If he ever completed his dissertation, *The Romantic Legacy: The Peasant Stories of Reymont, Hamsun, Laxness and Tolstoy,* what would happen to these books?

A fluorescent bulb flashed on some shelves away. The colors on the spines of the books seemed more vivid, sucking in any attention that came their way, like puppies pressing against a pet store window.

Ph.D. and dissertation in hand, he might be offered a slot in a university English department. Maybe the damn thing would be published by a third-rate university press, probably by the same school who'd hire him. Copies would be dutifully purchased by disinterested university librarians and shelved. There would be two reviews, both arrogant and unfavorable. The more hostile one would conclude, "His scholarship skates unevenly over the surface of these respected, if mainly minor, authors. Therefore, it is difficult to seriously consider his opinions when it is clear that neither the Polish nor the Icelandic works were read in the original."

These novels would sink back into oblivion, the acid in their pages causing each copy to self-destruct. Thirty years hence, his dissertation would yellow and crack as well.

He became stupefied with the pointlessness of it all, the utter indifference that his work would meet. It depressed him further knowing how much more work he had to do. Yet part of him, not blunted by the trivialization of scholarship, or worn down by the endless pressure to analyze, compare and explicate, loved these finely drawn visions of a simple life lived by decent people. It comforted him that their enemies were usually the forces of nature rather than the greed or pettiness of their fellow men.

That day, almost a year ago, stifled by the atmosphere in which he'd spent so many hours, he'd reached for *Independent People*, written, he knew, not in the rural Iceland of its setting but in the comfortable, sophisticated literary world of San Francisco. While writing it, however, Laxness had discovered to his chagrin that he was still an Icelander. Sweeps reread Bjartur's search for one of his small flock of sheep lost during a midwinter storm. Feeling, more than ever before, as if he were Bjartur, he suffered his chills, his numbness and his desperation. They stumbled and fell together, they fought against giving up; they continued the search. Together they rejoiced when he found the sheep. He felt fear as Bjartur fought to save the dull-witted sheep's life as well as his own from winter's freezing grip. He sighed with relief when the crofter returned to his dank sod hut, half-frozen, almost blind with fatigue, but triumphant.

Worn out, Sweeps closed the book. Gradually he became aware of the library: seasonless, timeless and silent. The musty smell, the darkness and the endless shelves of books, mostly left for dead, demoralized him. He wanted to live in these books, not write about them. He recalled Ed McClanahan, who taught creative writing, talking with him one hot afternoon. They were sharing a pitcher of dark beer at Zotts. "When someone calls you a fuckin' punk, you first got to see if they're right. If they are, you got to figure out how to get out of there." Sitting in the library, the last of his marijuana-augmented reflections ebbing away, Sweeps admitted he was far along on the path to fucking punkdom.

Those spring days, the more dope he smoked, the less he accomplished on the dissertation. When he smoked less, he did more work but became more depressed. If he smoked dope early in the day, he did no work at all but felt peaceful and content. When he smoked on a daily basis, he felt more guilty, as he did no work. He tried smoking just a little, intending to do no work. That felt wonderful.

One weekend he was stoned around the clock and read Heinlein's *Stranger in a Strange Land*. By Sunday night, his academic career, hanging together by a few threads, unraveled. He'd already dropped out, but no one, including himself, had acknowledged it.

That same week Randy's deferment came through. He was quitting nuclear engineering, a program, he told Sweeps, "that promised the worst of all possible worlds: opportunities to create new and better ways to leach the eyeballs off every living animal on the planet—and no job security."

"What'll you do now?" Sweeps asked.

"Hang out around here, smoke a little dope, drink beer and read a lot of science fiction till my rent deposit runs out. Then I'm driving to New Mexico. I can work on cars."

"Cars?"

"Everyone hates nuclear engineers. Everyone loves car mechanics."
Randy observed his distorted reflection in the beer glass he was holding.
"I'll stop at a commune. There's a bunch of them around Taos. I'll fix
their trucks, find me a fat chick who'll be grateful to be fucked by a
nerdy ex-engineer. Presto. I've got a life." He set the glass down and
cracked his knuckles. "Want to come?"

"I'm 2-S. Besides, I haven't any skills."

"You're right. Stick with literature."

Two months later, his 4-F card in his wallet, Sweeps left the Stanford
graduate program, taking with him the library's only copies of the books
he loved.

Eight months later, as far as he knew, the library hadn't noticed, had-
n't cared. He hadn't opened one of those novels for ages. On the shelf
above them stood his I Ching, Waite's Pictorial Key to the Tarot, The Tibetan Book of
the Dead, The Bhagavad-Gita, Underhill's The Spiritual Life, The Way of the Pilgrim, The
Life of Milarepa and Stranger in a Strange Land. The only immigrants who wandered up from his Stanford shelf to join these new volumes were Whitman and Dante. Something in him he could not name was nourished as
he looked over the titles. Maybe it was knowing that he was at the end of
a long line of people who'd been on this path before and had left these
gifts for others just beginning the walk.

CHAPTER 37

Eddie and Brad

Human nature
is not nearly as bad
as it has been thought to be.

Abraham Maslow

NITROUS EDDIE WAS ANGRY, something that startled everyone. Eddie was always Mr. Supercool, Joe Casual. He would sing out, "Hey man, it's all right!" to almost any situation. Even when strung out—a rare occurrence—he never complained. "Feeling fragile today" was the most negative state he'd admit to. So when he pounded up the steps and raced into the house shouting, "Evil! Fucking evil! I'm telling you, high-octane e-vile!" everyone paid attention.

Finnbar and Easy had been involved in an intense if one-sided conversation in the living room. Easy seemed to be listening earnestly, but he was deeply stoned, his mind wandering among pastel landscapes. He watched one soft wave of color displace another with slow and even majesty. Finnbar's words sounded like the fussing of an agitated squirrel and did nothing more than disturb the delicate colors.

A long silence, however, alerted Easy that he had better check in. He focused on Finnbar. "Really! Truly incredible, Finn," he said, an answer that usually encouraged Finnbar to resume talking.

But Finnbar had asked Easy if he was hungry. He was momentarily humiliated by Easy's absurd response, but Eddie's shouting distracted him from sliding into self-pity.

Startled by Eddie's vehemence, Sweeps glanced up from his book. Eddie, still shouting, came over to Finnbar, who winced and waved his hands in front of Eddie's face. "Down. Turn your volume down!"

"Sorry, man," Eddie said, his voice hushed and contrite. "I be cool." He arched up on his toes, sighed deeply and stretched until his fingertips brushed the hanging lamp. Then he crumpled to the rug, stunned into silence by his own disorientation.

Sweeps leaned over him. Eddie, his head on the rug, his legs sprawled, began to speak. "I'm walking by this house. This, this boob comes out: little glasses, pressed khaki pants, black loafers, matching socks. Being as nice as ever I can be, which is like to say so fucking nice I glow, I say, 'Hey man, if you have got a match I can make us both happier than a clam full of dip.' He says he has. 'Right on,' I say. I light up, take a fine first drag and pass him the joint. He takes a pee-pee-sized drag and tries to look cool. He fails so totally that I am starting to regret wasting even a single leaf of God's own on such. But, as is so often the case, my generosity overcomes my good sense. I say to him, 'Suck it up, man! Don't be a weenie! This is real quality shit.' He takes a deep drag which he imagines will cover up his deep squareness, but I have seen through his whole fucking act."

Sweeps sat back down and reopened his book. Easy became absorbed in watching Eddie's feet open and close like flippers. Only Finnbar was still listening.

"I start thinking maybe I could score some lunch. I lay that on him while he is breathing out. He says, 'Cough, cough, I have stuff for sandwiches inside' and takes another small drag. I say, 'I would rather you got it inside—me.' He laughs to show me that he is not totally without working brain cells, but still coughs and blows smoke at me through his teeth. I walk after him. But he is not about to let me past his door, a discourtesy that bums me out three thousand percent. I am left to sit on the step, wishing I was with real friends instead of this person who is so square he cannot roll over in bed." Eddie, impressed with his flair for description, stopped to admire his own words. The others made no response.

Sweeps, who was not listening to Eddie but could hardly keep from being aware of him, looked over when he went silent, wondering what could be important enough for Eddie to stop talking. When no one else spoke or even moved, Sweeps laid down his book and began to pay attention to Eddie's rambling.

Eddie went on. "He comes back out, almost trips over me, and drops the sandwich, which was no artwork to begin with. I pick up the bread and lettuce and cheese and slap it all back together. I offer him another toke which he is like reluctant to take 'cause it is so clear that I know he is an asshole. I say to him we should go to the park. I crave an infusion of green growing grass—'the beautiful uncut hair of graves.' He is as oblivious to my vast erudition as he is to everything else, but like a small dog, he wags his tail at the thought of a walk with yours truly. On the street when I lose traction he sets me upright. Like as not he's got mucho merit badges in old-lady-across-the-street-carrying affixed to the walls of his bedroom. We get to the park and hunker down against a tree, as he is, by now, not all that steady himself, groking that the stuff we are smoking is not bird droppings, but very fine, no seeds, no stems—primo, primo.

"After a few more inhalations, I am as friendly as one could be with a cat who so obviously has nothing going in his whole fucking life. He still looks kind of stupid, like Angelo used to. I make this comparison out loud. He freaks out and makes little wa-wa noises like he has shit in his pants. Fucking A if I have not hit a psychic home run. He's a former major league buddy of our same Angelo! I ask what he and Angelo were doing."

Eddie tried to sit up, failed and flopped down again. "He lays their whole scene on me, which, I am telling you directly, is putrid and repugnant!"

Eddie waved his arms about, breathed deeply and rubbed his hands on his chest as if he'd pulled something out of the air and wanted to absorb it. "No respect for women, no respect for drugs and fucking unpatriotic. Wipe their ass on the flag, the mothers."

Sweeps had previously pigeonholed Eddie as a stoned-out, good-hearted, street-smart idiot savant, the sort who gave drug taking a bad name. The remote possibility that Eddie had brain cells worth preserving was a revelation. Sweeps looked over at Finnbar, but he was staring at Eddie with the glassy gaze of someone listening to a foreign language.

"Try it again, Eddie, real slow," said Easy, who also was listening by now.

"Angelo was—and this cat, Brad-a-loo-loo, still is—assistant in the whorehouse, conning honest slobs with rusty cocks who arrive for a lube and oil. They take their brains out in salad dishes so that some little wormy guy can break Commie secret codes arising from the mud swamps in the Mekong Delta."

"Eddie, you're swinging at balls no one is pitching," Sweeps said.

Eddie flapped his feet and took a deep breath. "Weeks ago, I met two guys in the park, for whom I became their St. Bernard, leading them out of a very major lost-in-the-woods trip brought on by their inadvertent ingestion of sacred substances. I thought their heads had been unscrewed by gratuitous grace, but it was I, sagacious Eddie, finder of stoned persons, who didn't get it."

Finnbar said, "What are you talking about?"

"We gotta do something," Eddie said. "These streets are our garden on the freeway back to Eden. With snakes amongst us, how can we make honest parlance about the God-filled divinity that ennobles our every step, and to which we have pledged our dope-scoured, refried brains?"

Moonflower had come into the room. She wiped her hands on her jeans and said, "Eddie, it's all booga-booga coming out of your head. Why don't you cool out."

Seeing her face upside down, Eddie wasn't sure if she was frowning or smiling. That disconcerted him into a moment of silence. "Dirty dipshit is flowing out of that house," he began. No response. "Moon?" he whimpered.

"Stuff it, Eddie! Lie there till I feed you." Moonflower turned and walked out. The others left the room as well. Sprawled on the rug, Eddie worried how long he might be there, as he could not recall how to stand up.

By midnight, Eddie had come down enough to tell them what he'd learned. The drugs, the one-way glass, the night with Langwater. "There's right and there isn't. This isn't, and that's where I'm at."

Sweeps commented, "Schopenhauer says that if God created man to be miserable, he's done a fine job. Sadly enough, it is the nature of this world for injustice to be ascendent."

Easy said, "Maybe there's justice somewhere. But if there's not, we should make some." He brooded for several moments. "But what the hell—I got an idea."

CHAPTER 38

Shadow and Sweeps

Those of true wisdom and goodness
are contented to take persons and things as they are,
without complaining of their imperfections
or attempting to amend them.

Henry Fielding

"DO YOU LIKE ME?" Shadow was standing in Sweeps' doorway.
Sweeps stuck a finger in his book.

"Are you crazy?"

"Sure." She tossed her hair back. "But that's not my question. Do you like me?"

"Of course I like you." He reopened the book.

"But do you really?"

"What are you asking?"

Shadow rubbed one bare foot against her calf. "I mean—do you like me—all the way?"

Sweeps closed his book.

"I need to know," she said.

He sighed. "Well, sure. I mean, yes." He looked into her eyes.

"Angelo—"

"Angelo's dead."

"Hey—you all right?"

She wobbled through the door and practically fell on him. "No. I'm not! I'm sad and lonely, and I get scared."

He ran his hands up and down her spine as one might stroke a cat.

"Oh, Sweeps. Sleep with me. Love me."

"I couldn't."

"Yes, you could! You could. If you really really loved me."

Sweeps' hands rested gently on her back.

"Hold me tight! Touch me all over. Turn on to me." Her face was on his chest. "Not just fuck me, but really love me! That's what I want."

He stroked her hair. "Shadow. I—"

She thrust her head up. "If you don't, I'm going to go crazy." She dug her fingers into his neck. "Sometimes I want to die. I know it's stupid, babyish, bad soap opera." She laid her cheek back on his chest. "I want my life again."

The silence lengthened between them. "It wouldn't be right," he said, finally. "We both know that."

"Get out of your head, for Christ sake! Just once, get out of your head, your books, your brooms." She stroked one of his ears. "I'm not asking you to marry me. I just want to feel loved. Can you get hold of that?"

"I need to think."

"Thinkin's stinkin'! Thinkin's stinkin'," she sang out. She pulled his head down and kissed him. "Do I turn you on—at least a little?" She kissed him again and her tongue worked its way between his teeth. His arms tightened around her. "I do!" She clung to him, weeping and laughing. She kissed him again.

For a few moments as he lay kissing her, he allowed himself to admit how much he truly did care. What harm could come from loving someone he already loved? She was freaked out tonight, but tomorrow? No easy answer. He was being used. But what harm could come from it? He didn't know. Why not? Why the hell not?

Shadow's breath was warm in his ear. "Don't worry." She licked his neck. "I want us, us, us." She kissed his cheek. "I'll score a rubber from Moonflower. Oh, Sweeps! This is gonna be great."

She jumped up. "You're so—good." She blew him a loud kiss as she left the room. Sweeps sat forward on his mattress and shoved the door shut.

Maybe she won't come back, he half hoped. Moonflower will say something to deflect her. But she did return, her stuffed bear under her arm. In her hand, pressing into the bear's belly, he saw a packet of Trojans. She put the bear on his pillow. One of the bear's ears, missing its wire support, flopped down, covering a button eye.

"I don't think we should do this," Sweeps said.

"I'll tell you a secret," Shadow said, unfolding the fallen ear. "You think too much. Not only that," she said, sitting next to him, "you think too often. And—" she stretched out her arms, "you think wrong." She locked her fingers around his neck and kissed him. "Moonflower said, 'Ask Berry Bear.'"

She put her head on the pillow next to the bear. "Berry Bear, do you think he and I should? You know what I mean." She lifted up the fallen ear. "Oh? You think this is silly! A crush? Oh? I'm using him? Teenage melodrama?" She bit the erect ear. "You'd rather I stay with you. Sweet, sweet, sweet of you, but not tonight, Berry Bear. I love him. That makes it different. No, not forever and ever like I love you, but a whole big lot." She sat up, cocked her head to one side and stared at the bear. "All right for you, then." She picked the bear up and banished it to a corner of the bed, pushing its face against the wall.

"Berry Bear doesn't understand what human beings can do for each other." Her eyes started to tear. "Maybe it's because bears never need to forget."

In his mind, Sweeps saw an elderly professor standing at a blackboard. "The three variables are intimacy, passion and commitment," the professor explained. "The girl herself is clear that her commitment is shallow." He drew a short line. "Even less flattering, her passion is fleeting." He drew another short line. "Although she is aroused, however sexual the current context, her underlying demand is for intimacy. The summated vector can be represented thus."

Sweeps willed himself out of the classroom.

Shadow growled in his ear. "If you won't sleep with me, I'll find someone who will."

"Shouldn't we—"

Her hand went over his mouth. "Stop running the future. All we have is now! Only now, always it's now, forever now. If we're really free, we have to act free."

She kissed him fiercely. "Ooooh. Please, don't make me ask again." Shadow kicked back his covers. Sweeps felt waves of tenderness alternate with surges of desire. She unbuttoned his shirt and pulled it off. He stretched out a foot and pushed the door closed, heard the latch bolt scrape over the tip of the strike plate and click into place. Hyper-aware, he smelled her clean hair, felt the soft skin of her arm. A cup clinked against a plate in the kitchen. The trip handle of the toilet on the floor below clanged once, releasing the tank ball.

Shadow's ear rubbed against his rib cage. She eased out of his arms. She crawled down to the other end of the mattress, rolled his socks down to his ankles, pulled them over his heels and tugged them off. When she put her hand on his pants, he pushed it away and pulled her to him. They lay together, each wrapped around the other. "Let me get the lamp," he said. Since the switch was broken he had to pull the plug out of the wall socket. Her hands fumbled with his pants again before he lay back down.

"Don't lose control," he said.

"Why not?" She pulled his pants off and threw them to the far end of the mattress.

He pulled the blankets over them. "Are you cold?"

"Furthest thing from my mind," she said.

He edged a pillow under her head.

"Would you do one more thing for me?" she asked in a purr.

"More than likely."

She climbed astride him, put her fists on her hips and said, "Stop talking!"

He raised his face and nodded so that his nose caressed her lips. He lifted her nightie off and threw it toward his pants. She rolled off him and joined him under the covers. He reached over. For a moment she resisted his pull. She placed her hand on his chest. "I wanted to be with you, just to do it, from the day you picked me up—after Thomas' party. Did you know?"

He shook his head.

"Only, that day, I didn't want anyone touching me. Thomas fucked me the night before. I felt too dirty."

He continued to caress her cheek.

"Should I stop talking?"

"Yes," he said in a whisper. Her fingers touched a small patch of hair in the center of his chest.

Angelo, baby, please understand! Try!

Sweeps kissed her moist eyes closed.

CHAPTER 39

Easy's mission

Our government will realize the necessity
of telling people the truth.
Times are coming
when the government will need
the complete confidence of all citizens
if this country is to endure.

Ernest Hemingway

EASY BECAME INCREASINGLY BUSY and furtive. He took to wearing camouflage pants and refusing to answer to any name but C. C., which he said meant Command and Control. Only after Eddie had sworn a hundred different ways that he could be trusted did Easy take him into his confidence.

Afterwards, Eddie ran all over the house shouting, "Loose lips sink ships" before lapsing into complete silence. He ran his fingers over his lips again and again as if renewing the glue that would keep them shut. He put his fingers over everyone else's lips as well, except Moonflower's. When he reached out toward her mouth, she slapped his hand away. "Put those dirty little paws on me and I'll learn you about loose balls!" Eddie

218

clutched his crotch and scurried away.

Three nights later, Easy and Eddie walked in, hefting fully loaded backpacks, which they took into the cellar. Emerging, Easy called the whole house together. "This is it," he said. "I need everyone. Tomorrow, at four hundred hours, we move out. Wear regular clothes—no costumes, watches, rings or beads."

Behind him, Eddie chinned strong agreement up and down.

Shadow stood up. "I don't want to play."

Sweeps and Moonflower looked at each other. Easy folded his arms and said in a quiet voice, "You'll miss a high time, a very high time."

Shadow looked away. "I'm sure you all can get it on without me." She walked out of the room. No one spoke for a moment. Looking around at the rest of them, Easy scratched his beard. "No time to cry over split broads. Anyone else copping out?"

"I mean, is it all right what we're doing?" Finnbar asked.

Easy made no response. Eddie rolled his eyes and moaned.

Finnbar spoke again. "Is it legal?"

Eddie exploded. "Listen, Finnface. In a world where it's legal and jolly patriotic to bomb and scorch yellow people's children, legal's hollow pigshit. Don't lay your twit moral code on me or I'll—"

Easy turned on him. "You're still under orders."

Eddie sputtered back into silence.

Easy spoke again. "At ease, all of you. Get some shut-eye before we move out. Eddie will take the first watch." Easy paused, staring directly at Eddie. "And if you smoke anything, I'll cut one of your balls off."

Easy then vanished into the cellar. Finnbar, having decided not to go back to the church to sleep, went upstairs with Moonflower. After a few minutes, Sweeps drifted off to his room.

Soon after, Easy came up the cellar stairs carrying a large cloth sack. Eddie let him out the front door. In a half-hour, Easy was back empty-handed. At two o'clock he woke Eddie, who was snoring lightly in a chair, and told him to stretch out. Easy prowled around the house until he satisfied himself that everyone was asleep. Then he brought a number of small parcels up from the cellar and stuffed them into the pockets of an oversize combat jacket.

At five minutes to four, he tapped on their doors. "Living room. Five minutes. It's a go!"

Bleary but excited, they assembled. Easy wore his camouflage pants, and the bulky jacket over a black turtleneck sweater. Eddie spoke to everyone. "We all follow C. C., but in little groups, like we're out late and not with each other."

"Finnbar," said Easy, "are you a chickenshit or a gladiator? Chickenshits stay home."

Finnbar took his glasses off and wiped them clean. "How about sword carrier—third class?" Eddie walked over and gave him a bear hug. Finnbar was so pleased his eyes momentarily went out of focus. He had to touch his glasses to be sure they were on.

Easy quietly told each person what he expected of them. "I'll review it on site. No mistakes!"

Eddie opened the door. Easy led and the rest followed. They walked out into a night that was cool and without a breeze. Moonflower fell in stride with Finnbar.

Easy walked firmly, with a casual yet steady stride, seemingly oblivious to everyone he passed. In minutes they were all assembled across the street from the house where Angelo had worked. Except for a single light on the whorehouse porch, both buildings were dark.

Easy took a five-inch switchblade from one pocket and snapped it open. From another, he extracted a tiny flashlight. He handed both to Finnbar. Out of the opposite pocket came a wire cutter and a second flashlight, which went to Sweeps. Eddie was handed a box of matches. Easy fished out two more small flashlights, passing one to Eddie and holding the other.

"Finn. That house over there." He pointed to the house next to the staff house. "Ease open the side gate—the latch is on top. About twenty feet in, there's a coiled hose. Cut it partway through, about three feet from the faucet end. If their dog barks, just keep slicing. If lights go on, get out." Easy cracked his knuckles. Finnbar jumped at the sound.

"Sweeps. Go up on the porch to the far right end. You'll need to stand on the railing. Hold the flashlight in your mouth. At eye level you'll see two wires. Cut the lower one; it's the phone. The upper is the power line. If you cut the wrong wire, it will fry you and flip you into the street. Remember, clip the lower one. Then climb back down. Don't jump! And walk down the stairs like you live there."

Sweeps nodded. He looked into the lens of the tiny flashlight and turned it on. Easy grabbed it away. "Like this." He covered the lens with his hand, thumbed it on for a second and clicked it off. He handed it back.

Moonflower still stood at Easy's side. "Moonflower," he said. "When we've all gone across, keep an eye out. If anyone stops and looks at us, dance."

"Dance?"

"Yeah! Shake your things. And holler like a crazy lady." He looked at everyone. "If she hoots, freeze where you are. I'll create a diversion if Moonflower's not enough."

"Trust me, honey," Moonflower said in her most sultry voice.

Sweeps fingered the wire cutter nervously. "You and Eddie?"

Easy grinned. "You'll see." He put his hands on his hips and leaned back, taking them all in. "You'll do. You'll do just fine." He squatted on his heels. "This should take no more than two, three minutes max—if you're slow." A car came down the street. Easy didn't move until it was half a block past them.

"Don't be slow." He cracked his knuckles again. "Moon, make like a streetwalker, back and forth, just to draw any eyes that might drive by."

"What if some guy decides he wants me?"

"Tell him a hundred bucks. That'll keep him moving."

"C. C.," she said, "this better be good."

"Smoother than silver," Easy said.

Easy checked the street and waved them across. Finnbar and Sweeps reached the opposite curb first, Eddie and Easy three feet behind them. Easy watched Finnbar ease open the gate, then beckoned to Eddie. Together, they opened the gate on the side of the staff house and crept into the side yard.

Easy pulled a candle out of his coat and fitted it into a paper cup. "Watch where I put these. When I get the third one set, you start after me. Light the candles. After you light one, spit on the match and put it in your pocket. Don't drop it! Touch anything with the match but the candle, and you're in trouble. Light 'em, then get back out! Got it?"

Eddie nodded.

Easy crawled under the house. A flick of his flashlight showed Eddie where he'd placed the first candle. Almost invisible, Easy moved again. A second flick of light. A pause. Then a third. Trying to remember the location of the first candle, Eddie came within two feet of it before he needed the light. He struck a match and brought it toward the candle. A light breeze blew it out. He put the dead match in his pocket. Chilled and sweating, he lit a second. This time it flickered but stayed lit until he touched it to the exposed wick. It caught. He squeezed the match head with his fingers, burned himself, took the flashlight out of his mouth, spit on his fingers and carefully put the match into his pocket. The first candle gave enough light for him to locate the second, perched on a beam about four feet from the edge of the house. He crawled over to it and lit the second candle on his first try.

The third candle was much farther away, near the other edge of the house. Eddie had to crouch to reach it. He used up three matches before it caught. The third match almost burned into his hand. It was all he could do not to run around the edge of the house.

Back across the street, everyone was waiting.

"All lit?" Easy asked.

"Piece of cake," said Eddie, shaking.

"Good work!"

"Finn?"

"I cut it. But the dog started barking."

"You did all right," Easy said. Moonflower squeezed Finnbar's arm.

"Sweeps?"

"Wire's cut."

"We're in good shape," Easy said, his voice even. "Now the fun part." He reached into the recesses of his coat.

"There's more?" Finnbar asked.

"Finn," Eddie said. "You think we came just to bless the place?"

"That's what he said we were going to do."

"C. C. said consecrate, and that's what we're about to do," Eddie said. "We're going to transubstantiate this motherfucker."

Easy looked over at Finnbar. "Forgive me, Father, for I know ass-kissing well what I do." He pulled a polished steel slingshot from his pocket and slipped a wide rubber strap into its side slots. Reaching into a side pocket, he took out four metal balls the size of marbles.

"What are those?" Moonflower asked.

"Ball bearings for airplane wheels," Easy said. "Uncle Sam cares, Uncle Sam shares." He straightened his jacket and strode across the street.

"I don't get it," Finnbar said.

Easy put a ball bearing in the slingshot and opened the gate. He stepped in, took aim, pulled and released. A loud thunk reverberated from under the house. Across the street, Finnbar blew on his fingers.

Easy reloaded. Another thunk. He stood motionless—for a full minute. Then he stretched out his arms and turned around. Once, twice, three times. Then, like an archer, he pulled the rubber band back. With a single smooth gesture, he pivoted on one heel, raised the slingshot and released the ball. The "wang" of the rubber strip and a clink followed so close that the two seemed to be a single sound. Across the street, they all held their breath.

From under the porch, flames flared out with a loud whoosh. Easy moved to the other side of the house and, crouching, let fly another shot. Another wang-clink and a second whoosh. The far side of the house erupted in flames.

Easy ran back to the others. "Damn. I missed the middle one both times."

"Jesus, what was under the candles?" asked Sweeps.

"Gauze rolls and piles of cotton soaked in jet fuel—leaves no traces."

Finnbar was transfixed by the flames. "We're murdering them!"

Easy's hand came down hard on his shoulder. "Didn't I tell you? I don't kill people—anymore. Count to ten, real slowly. Then you can yell fire. All of you."

Easy moved back across the street to the whorehouse. As Finn reached the count of ten, Easy sent a ball bearing through the second-floor bay window, shattering the center pane.

"Fire," Finnbar yelled, flapping his arms.

"Fire," Easy shouted, and took out another window with a second shot.

"Fire!" Moonflower shrieked, louder than both men together. The first broken window lit up.

Sweeps ran and stood under it. "Fire. Fire, fire!" he yelled. A woman's head appeared. "Fire next door, ma'am—thought you'd like to know," he said.

"Holy shit!" the woman said, and vanished. Other lights snapped on. Shrill yelling could be heard throughout the house.

The crawl space below the staff house burned vigorously, flames blowing in every direction. Easy raced up the sidewalk. He stopped, and aiming carefully, began blasting out the house's upper windows.

An upstairs window opened. Bear appeared, gun in hand, its barrel rose colored, reflecting the flames below. Easy moved deep into the shadows. The front door of the whorehouse flew open. Girls in robes stumbled down the steps. The madame, who had gone out the back, ran around and met them.

Easy slowly raised his slingshot. He pulled back on the rubber band and, holding his breath, released it. The steel ball struck Bear's hand. The gun bounced off the sill and hit the ground three feet from where Easy stood. Still hugging the shadows, he kicked it into the flames. Then he backed out to the street and, waving to the others, streaked across. They followed as quickly as they could.

As Easy's feet touched the opposite curb, a series of muffled explosions erupted under the house. He dropped to the pavement, but a moment later was back up.

Brad was the first one out of the house. Across the street, Eddie saw him and stepped back out of sight. Lou followed Brad. The rest of the staff emptied out behind them. Bear came last, holding his wrist and swearing. He limped on the edge of one bare foot. "Get a hose," he roared.

Next door the lights had come on. A dog barked furiously. Its owner, already outside, raced to turn on his hose. When he did, water burst from the cut Finnbar had made.

Easy dashed over. "Turn it on the fire," he yelled.

"I can't!" the man said. "It's split."

"Wet down your own house then, man! Use your thumb. Save your home!"

The man picked up the hose at the cut and turned it on his own house. The walls of the staff house flared and crackled behind him. Easy returned to the group across the street.

Lights were on everywhere. Shouting warnings to one another, neighbors found their garden hoses and sprayed portions of the staff house, but none of the water could reach the center of the conflagration. By the time the first fire engine arrived, the front porch had fallen in on itself.

After the flames pierced the ground floor, the staircase became a funnel pulling the fire up behind it. In moments, it was everywhere. The firemen snaked out their hose. After a few seconds of consultation, they turned it on the closest wall of the whorehouse, wetting it down thoroughly before turning to the staff building.

Across the street Easy, Sweeps, Eddie, Finnbar and Moonflower mingled with the growing crowd. Flo, wrapped in a yellow and black silk kimono, stood near Eddie. "You live there?" he asked.

"What's it to you?"

"Sorry, babe. Just being civil to a fellow creature."

An elderly woman stood next to Moonflower. "Such a place!" she said in a Middle European accent. "Bad girls dere, you hippies everyvere and now dis. Dis neighborhood not vort shit no more!"

Bear stood in the street watching the water play up and down the walls. He grimaced when a piece of the roof fell in with a loud crack. Within ten minutes the house was a smoldering ruin, the air filled with the smell of wet burnt wood.

Easy made a clicking sound in his throat. Less than ten feet away, Eddie turned. Easy turned his back and walked away. Eddie tapped Sweeps. They started off in the same direction. Finnbar and Moonflower, arms around each other, ambled off the other way.

From across the street, Brad looked over. Eddie twisted his hips and limped away, pushing his stomach out, trying to look as unlike himself as possible. Brad turned away. The staff gathered around Bear. Nearby, the whores, in multicolored robes, clustered together like a flock of large tropical birds.

CHAPTER 40

The humbling of Nitrous Eddie

Along the way to knowledge,
Many things are accumulated.
Along the way to wisdom,
Many things are discarded.

Lao-tzu

REUNITED AND FLUSHED WITH EXCITEMENT, the troop turned the corner and marched up Clayton Street toward the house.

"Shit, man, you put me in mortal danger," Eddie said, as he walked beside Easy. "If I'd dropped my match under there, I'd have been flash-crisped. This very bag of skin to which I have become passionately attached faced potential premature termination."

"You didn't need to know," Easy said.

"How can you stay so cool?" Sweeps asked, putting his hand on Easy's shoulder.

Easy shook Sweeps' hand off and looked straight ahead. "I'm on horse."

Moonflower whirled to face him. "You shot up? Oh, my clear blue

Jesus."

"Just one hit—for Angelo."

"Wow!" Moonflower said.

They all fell silent. Then Moonflower started singing. "Hi ho, hi ho." Everyone but Easy joined in. "It's home from work we go." They whistled and made little trumpet sounds, then lapsed into laughter.

Eddie turned to Finnbar. "Nothing like an early morning pagan-burning to give one an appetite. Like being on special assignment for the Inquisition, n'est-ce pas?"

"I'm glad it's over," Finnbar said.

"So am I," Sweeps said.

Finnbar sighed. "Every time I'm with you people, something terrible happens." He put his hands in his pockets and sucked in his cheeks. "I hope Christ will consider these as very unusual circumstances."

"A good test case," Sweeps said. "If Christ doesn't treat you right, come over to Buddha-land. Lots of heavens, lots of room, lifetimes to clean up your act."

Eddie reached out and patted Easy's pockets. "Easy, old ice man, would you pass your lethal weapon to an openhearted fellow destroyer? Armed with rubber and steel, I could rid our neighborhood of its remaining undesirable elements: tourists in short pants, narcs passing as honest drug dealers, anyone else who would limit our deity-derived right to explore alternate realities. I'll snap the strap of your stone-flinger at every man, woman or pig who retards planetary liberation, and protect us from the conspiracy of both lower chakra political parties whose elephant and donkey shit litters these streets." Eddie held his hands out.

"No," said Easy.

The dagger-like intensity of the refusal rendered Eddie silent, but just for a moment. "So Eddie's not high enough on your list of merry men to fuck in your forest." He stopped and scuffed the toe of one shoe on the sidewalk. "Good enough to get his behind blowtorched, but not enough moxie to make it into the peacetime safety and surveillance corps." Eddie hunched his shoulders, then walked around and addressed Easy's other side.

"Why then did you pick me as your trusted aide? I had imagined—foolish and vain as this now appears—it was for the remarkable acuity of my pupils, naturally enlarged by their constant exposure to vision-expanding chemicals, coupled with my exceptional manual dexterity which, had I been born in a more sensible, sane and sagacious century, could have led to a successful career as a touring juggler. Plus, of course, my flexible mind, which, even though it compromises my deeply felt and often touted humility, is ever able to discard and replace ideas, even deeply rooted preconceptions."

"You were my third choice," Easy said.

"Oh," Eddie said, putting one hand to his cheek as if he'd been slapped. "Not only does Nitrous Eddie offer his heart, open as an Aztec sacrificial victim, later to be made aware that a single stumble would have resulted in his ass turning pot-roast brown. Now he garners the reward for the utter perfection of his heroic action: a dose of ego reduction as unwelcome as crotch control to a horny rabbit."

Walking backward in front of Easy, Eddie began to bob and weave like a boxer. "Sweeps was my first choice," Easy said. "But I didn't think he'd crawl under there. Shadow was my second. You were what was left."

Eddie stopped dancing and fell back into step.

"Eddie, I told you before we went out that if you smoked, I'd cut off one of your balls," Easy said in the same even tones. "Are you not stoned now?"

"Ay, ay, mon Capitaine, you did," Eddie said, veering out of reach. "Although I was sorely tested by my own carnal nature to take a few tokes, as severely as was St. Anthony in the desert by all the minions of Satan, yet I did not. Tormented as well by my own personal knowledge that such an ingestion would make me more vigilant and clear-eyed, I reviewed your unasked-for offer to separate one testicle from its partner and manfully foreswore any form of infusion."

Eddie snapped to attention and put his hand to his forehead in a ges-ture that bore only the most distant resemblance to a military salute.

"Sergeant Major, I did not so much as lick the end of the partly smoked high-quality joint that I did have, in point of fact, sitting in my buttoned chambray shirt pocket. After the target structure became a col-orful and pleasing display against the dawn-speckled sky, improving, al-beit briefly, the general dreariness of the neighborhood, and after we'd all run about like town criers lauding the burning of Rome, I deter-mined, operating on my own recognizance, as I was trained to do in the hemp fields in which I was raised, sir—" Eddie attempted another salute, "that the military portion of our campaign had come to an end. And that part of our cover—which included Nitrous Eddie, totally out of character, unstoned, and steady as a high-wire artist—no longer served our stated objectives. I thus elected to resume my normal identity, but in a way that would not contravene your orders and therefore would not bring upon me the retribution you'd suggested would transpire should I have disobeyed, which, in this case, I most certainly did not."

Easy looked at him quizzically. Eddie's eyes, bathed in innocence, looked back, pupils wide and dark. "Mon Général, I ate the whole joint."

Easy looked away and Eddie did not see his face soften into a smile.

Sensing that he was out of danger, Eddie brightened. "Thus, like a Baptist after an H-two-O immersion or a squirrel after an acorn binge, I now feel restored to resume my flowing, flowering life, more attuned to the vibes of trees and angels than to the vengeful militaristic attack-and-fire bomb team of which I so recently was the pivotal member."

"If they could bottle you, I'd drink you," Moonflower said.

"Plugged would be my choice—sealed shut with the seal of Solomon and thrown into the sea for a thousand-thousand quiet years," Sweeps said.

Eddie heard none of these remarks. He had stepped into a doorway and was talking animatedly to the closed door.

They trooped into the house. "I'll wake Shadow," Moonflower said. "We're going to have ourselves one hell of a party. She, by rights, is the guest of honor."

The others flocked into the kitchen. A moment later, Moonflower came back downstairs. "She's not here. She's gone."

CHAPTER 41

God opens doors

Now that my storehouse
has burned down,
nothing conceals the moon.

Masahide

SHADOW HAD AWAKENED a dozen times during the night. She was no more than half asleep when Easy roused the others. She stayed awake, listening. She heard the stairs creak and their voices until the front door closed.

She got up and got dressed, felt her way slowly down the stairs and through the dark hall. Only after she was in the living room did she turn on a light. She turned it on and off twice before sitting down cross-legged on the couch. In less than a minute, there was a light tap on the front door. She parted it a crack, then threw it open.

"Thanks for waiting," she said to the group standing on the porch.

"We got to watch the moon set," Alonzo said.

"And see the stars," Maya added.

Shadow held the door open for them to enter.

"I don't have much stuff," Shadow said.

"Any amount is okay with us. Our space es su space," Trevor said, sitting on the couch.

Maya's arms went around Shadow. "Need any help?" The two ascended the stairs hand in hand.

Shadow had sorted everything into piles. On top of one stood her beach bag, filled to overflowing. Shadow pointed to a small ear sticking out of the bag. "Berry Bear doesn't like to travel much. I put him in there so he'd feel snug."

Maya rubbed Shadow's arm. "What made you decide?"

"Can't tell you." She shrugged. "Don't know myself that well. Ask me why not."

"Okay—why not?"

"My bridges are all burned." She picked up the beach bag. "So why not? Can you take this pile? The other is all giveaways."

Maya followed her down the stairs carrying a bundle of clothes and a dozen records. Shadow held the beach bag, a jacket and a pillow. Trevor took them from her and walked out to the car.

"Do they know?" Maya asked.

"No! I couldn't take any more leavings."

Maya looked at her but said nothing.

"Not real brave, huh? I'm not feeling real brave right now. I left notes and my part of the rent and stuff. I'm clean with everyone."

"It's your drama," Maya said, with a tiny shrug.

Shadow looked around the living room. "I love them all." She straightened the throw rug and fluffed up the couch cushions. "But it's time for me to go." She walked around the room and turned off the lights.

"Where is everyone?" asked Maya.

"Out. But they can't bring him back. Oh, Maya," Shadow said. "I wanted it all to be different." She tried to control her sobbing. Maya hugged her tightly.

"For a while it was. It really was." Shadow stepped back and wiped her eyes.

Maya sang softly. "Welcome to this universe in which you are the star."

Shadow looked up the stairs, and back to Maya. "Then I'm bringing down the curtain. Please! Let's go, before they come back."

A red VW bus, packed to the windows, stood at the curb. "God Squad" in sweeping white letters decorated one side; a series of breaking blue and white waves covered the other. Shadow climbed in and curled up in the far back.

As the bus crossed the Bay Bridge, she fell asleep. She was still asleep when they turned south on Route 99 and headed toward Fresno. The band was scheduled to play one night there at the Pigs and Fifth before driving to Phoenix, where they would open for Big Brother and the Holding Company at the Rising Son Be-In.

In Fresno, Shadow did her share of unloading and setting up, quickly becoming just another member of the crew.

"What do you mean gone!" Sweeps shouted, running in from the kitchen.

"What the fuck do you think she means? Gone, scrammed, scadoodled, split." Eddie had the refrigerator door open and was pulling out cheese and the remains of a small salami. "Before her natural tendency towards effusive gratitude might have showed itself to me, the little darling ups and takes a powder," he said to the interior of the refrigerator. He moved to the kitchen table and laid the food out. "I was prepared to recount for her my bold steps onto the scales of justice while I ogled her flesh." He set out plates and napkins.

Sweeps looked down at him. "You're disgusting."

"Years of practice," Eddie said.

Moonflower, sitting on the stairs, waved a piece of paper. "This was on her stuff." She read it, then let it drop to the floor.

"What does it say?" asked Easy.

"Nothing but 'Give these things to the free store, most of it came from there' and 'Tell the guys at the Trip Shop everything's cool.'"

"That's it?" Sweeps asked.

"That's all she wrote," Moonflower said.

"Fucking ingrate," Eddie said cheerfully. "Suicides leave you a better note. Give that girl a zero on savoir faire." He looked at everyone. "I share your general feeling of having been kicked somewhere below the buckle, but I, at least, have the good sense to be stoned. Thus, in spite of sorrow and surprise," he gestured to the food before him, "my appetite is undiminished. Them that has, eats. Marxism one-o-one. Them that hungers after righteousness don't eat as good nor as often. Christianity one-o-one."

That night when Moonflower pulled her nightshirt out from under her pillow, she found another note.

> I love you.
> I want you to be the biggest success in the whole world!
> And have lots of guys just pant for you (ruf-ruf-ruf).
> I'll be cheering for you
> wherever I am.

Under the rolled-up sweater he used as a pillow, Sweeps found a letter. He held it a long time before unfolding it.

> You are the best person I know (honest).
> I'm being carried away by folks who'll take care of me almost as good as you.
> Tell my folks everything.
> I left 100's of kisses just for you. Don't use them up too fast.
> Your little dancer.

Sweeps read the letter again, then set it down beside him. He looked at his books, leaned over and pulled down the I Ching. He opened it at random. On page 493 he read,

"Nine in the fifth place.
a) Men bound in fellowship first weep and lament
But afterward they laugh.
After great struggles they succeed in meeting."

In a curious way that he did not fully understand, he felt comforted, as if whatever he had done was acceptable in the eyes of the universe.

Two days later, about nine in the evening, there was a loud knocking at the front door. Easy opened it to a uniformed police officer. "Good evening, officer. Any problems on the beat this lovely evening?"

"A girl name of Lollie Anne live here?"

"Lollie Anne? No, sir," Easy said, starting to close the door. "No one by that name."

The policeman stopped the door with his foot. "Hold it, sonny. She's also called Shadow or Dancer."

"Oh? I shall ask." He turned, blocking the doorway with his body, and yelled. "Anybody living here named Shadow Dancer? Nice police officer standing right here with me wants to know."

Everyone crowded into the hall.

"Is she in trouble?" Moonflower asked.

"That all depends," the officer said. They waited for him to speak. He moved farther into the house. "I got her folks here. The kid's a runaway." He waved at the police car parked at the curb. Another policeman got out, followed by a middle-aged couple.

"Don't any of you try to get smart with us." As he entered the house, the man eyed them with distaste. "Lollie Anne called home three nights ago and told us where she was."

Sweeps stepped forward. "She told you the truth. She lived here." He beckoned them toward the living room. They all followed him in.

The two policemen and the couple stood in the center of the living room. Sweeps sat on the couch and faced them.

"We'll tell you about your daughter." He gestured to include the others standing in the doorway. "You may not realize it, but you're among friends."

Afterword

The line between truth and fiction is often hard to discern, especially when recalling and re-creating an era often described as "if you remember it, you weren't there."

It was true that "The Agency" funded and ran a whorehouse in San Francisco and that it was used as a laboratory to observe how subjects would react to being given LSD and other drugs without their knowledge. It is also true that the same agency at the same time was funding research and conferences about LSD by funneling money through non-profit foundations. For this novel, I moved the whorehouse across town, but since the Agency hardly wishes to claim credit for the research program, I expect I will be forgiven. The code name for the actual research program (which I didn't use, as it would have seemed too outlandish) was "Operation Midnight Climax."

The Be-In occurred almost exactly as presented. It was the first time that the political revolutionaries, fighting against the war and other social injustices, met the hippies, who were not, at that time, fighting for anything other than the right to be left alone.

The Candy Man's character is fictional, but not so what he and others were doing that day.

The song titles and lyrics by the God Squad are all unrecorded creations of a group out of Santa Cruz that called themselves the Fun Band. All the fictional characters are my own creation.

In a work of nonfiction, it is usual to acknowledge all the people who helped, whose ideas you appropriated and those who actually worked with you to beat the manuscript into shape. There is a conspiracy of silence about fiction writing, however, as if an author steps into a windowless office and emerges months or years later with a polished and distinctive work of art. Nothing could be farther from the truth.

I owe debts of gratitude to too many people to list, but at least I can acknowledge the writing group led by Shelly Lowenkauf and Leonard Tourney that I've been part of for many years. And a deep bow to my father William and stepmother Regina Fadiman, who read the first awkward drafts and did not advise me to seek out another line of work.

My editor at Celestial Arts, Tom Southern, reignited my excitement in completing this book. My wife, Dorothy, waylaid this manuscript as I was sending it out and polished it yet one more time. Sarah Nawrocki, the text editor, corrected countless small errors and suggested many felicitous word changes. Not to be outdone, Judy Bloch, the proofreader, sanded every line smooth.

Several years ago, a senior editor at a major New York publishing house assured me that while The Other Side of Haight was a fine novel, there was no market for '60s fiction. I asked Jeremy Tarcher, a distinguished publisher in his own right, what the editor meant. He said, "The East Coast didn't understand the '60s when they were happening. They still don't."

I can appreciate their point of view. The explorers and adventurers of the '60s made every traditional institution in the country take stock of itself. While the conservative establishment keeps trying to discredit the social gains achieved, the fact is that the progress in civil rights, women's rights, environmental awareness, acceptance of non-Christian religions, respect for Native Americans, et cetera, has come, at least in part, from those sandaled, pot-smoking, wide-eyed, sexually fumbling, kind and generous, naive and often misguided hippies world-wide who were willing to take a chance with their lives to make this world a better place.

Did we make mistakes? Endlessly. But we set into motion forces that are still working to heal this planet and help each other to be a more humane species.

Days before his premature death from brain cancer, Terence McKenna, one of the great explorers of inner space, said,

> Everything is a blessing and everything comes as a gift. And I don't regret anything about the situation I find myself in. If psychedelics don't ready you for the great beyond, then I don't know what really does. . . .
>
> I have an absolute faith that the universe prefers joy and distills us with joy. That is what religion is trying to download to us, and this is what every moment of life is trying to do—if we can open to it.

It's a privilege to honor those who opened up the path that some of us are still travelling. Thanks to all my friends, living and dead, who have supported and inspired this book.

—James Fadiman
Palo Alto, 2000

For more about this novel, the characters, the facts in the fiction, the era, the music, the events, more photos by Elaine Mayes, and links to the Haight itself, check out my website:

www.othersideofhaight.com